"I'm offering you a job, Miranda."

Miranda glared back fiercely at Blake. "Are you?" she challenged. "I think you just want to keep me here."

"That, too. Out of my sight you seem to get yourself into considerable trouble. Of course," he went on, ignoring her furious gasp, "if you need excitement I'm willing to supply it. Anything to keep you on the right track. An admirable situation, don't you think? You teach little Andrea and I'll teach you...."

"No, thanks! I've had enough lessons from you!" Miranda tried to turn away, but he caught her swiftly about the waist.

Blake's blue gaze pierced her. "Life is all lessons," he told her coolly. Then he drew her firmly back against him, and his strong arms encircled her like a cage....

Home to Morning Star

by

MARGARET WAY

Harlequin Books

TORONTO • LONDON • LOS ANGELES • AMSTERDAM
SYDNEY • HAMBURG • PARIS • STOCKHOLM • ATHENS • TOKYO

Original hardcover edition published in 1981
by Mills & Boon Limited

ISBN 0-373-02490-8

Harlequin edition published July 1982

CHAPTER ONE

THE telephone woke her, shrilling out in the hall-way.

'Yes?' she said huskily, one arm in, the other out of her embroidered, pink crêpe-de-chine peignoir.

'Miss Seymour? Herriot and Associates here. Mr Herriot to speak to you.'

'Thank you.' Miranda covered the phone with her hand and yawned delicately. Why would George be ringing at such an ungodly hour?

'Miranda?' It was George Herriot's voice, rich and plummy.

' 'Morning, George.'

'You sound sleepy, m'dear. Another party?'

'Just dinner with Shane.'

'Ah yes.' George didn't like Miranda's newest fiancé. 'Fact is, m'dear, I'd like to see you some time this morning.'

'Can't it wait, George?' She had an appointment at the hairdresser's at eleven, then lunch with Shane. The new place, Allegra.

'No, m'dear, it can't!' George affected a firm tone. 'Shall we say ten-thirty *sharp*?'

Put on her mettle, Miranda arrived right on time. George came towards her, portly and genial, his small, twinkly blue eyes musing over her youthful chic. 'Ravishing!' he commented with almost paternal pride. 'What a pretty girl you are, Miranda. Sometimes makes me wish I'd overcome my aversion to marriage. I'd have enjoyed a daughter like you.'

'But you've been like a father to me, George,' Miranda said affectionately.

'God knows I've tried.' George shook his downy head with the gleaming bald patch. 'To think Marcy had to hare off to America and leave you at home.'

Miranda sank down upon George's deep leather armchair, adjusting the skirt of her canary yellow dress. 'We've been through this before, George. I love the States, but I much prefer home. We have a great way of life; the informality and the freedom. My heart and spirit are here, George.'

'Yet your mother spent the last five years of her life in California.'

'I was never lonely!' Miranda protested. 'I loved school and university. I have plenty of friends.'

'That tends to happen when one is considered wealthy.'

'Isn't it lovely!' Miranda agreed complacently. 'I can't believe Marcy's gone. She was so incredibly vivacious.'

'She was that!' George very nearly clicked his tongue. Marcy Seymour had been quite the scattiest woman he had ever known, but so exquisite, so utterly free from vanity or malice, one could have forgiven her anything. One *did*. Even the near-desertion of her only child. Her untimely death at the age of forty-four had been quite in keeping with her high-spirited way of life. Where other women remained quietly looking after their homes and families, Marcy had taken up hang-gliding. To her cost.

'So what is it?' Miranda was disconcerted to see George looking so upset. 'The will, George,' she prompted. 'Is that what's bothering you, you old softie? No need to read it out. Just tell me how much I've got.'

George almost flinched. 'My darling girl, I find myself almost weeping. There's nothing!'

'Come off it, George.' What a time for George to thinking of making jokes!

'It's true, m'dear.' George took off his glasses to polish them. 'Marcy was incredibly foolish. She was always financing one or other of that gigolo's harebrained schemes. It didn't seem to occur to her that he had no talent and even less of a head for business than she. The upshot is, there's nothing left.'

Shock turned Miranda's flawless young skin paper-white. 'I don't believe it!' she said blankly, her mind refusing to encompass the serious consequences of what George was saying. 'Why, Daddy left Marcy a fortune!'

'Which she frittered away on gee-gaws and gigolos!' George pursed his pink lips. 'Even fortunes run out,' he observed wryly. 'Though I told her and *told* her, Marcy always thought Seymour money inexhaustible. In fact she devoted most of her enormous energy towards spending it. She and that . . . *feller* she married.' He sighed deeply. 'Not even a respectable, mature man, but a bit player in low-grade movies.'

'But he was terribly handsome, George, wasn't he?' Miranda said fairly. 'Marcy's real priority was a good-looking man before money.'

'A bloody gigolo!' George said intolerantly.

'Why, he even bullied her!'

'Marcy loved having rows,' Miranda pointed out, never in any doubts about her mother. She lifted her trembling hands and looked at them. Shane's ring, a solitaire diamond, flashed so brightly she winced. 'Whatever is he going to do without Marcy?'

'Marry another rich woman ten years his senior!' George ripped out waspishly. 'I beseeched Marcy not to marry him, but as usual she never listened. She just succumbed to that brawny numbskull. No wonder the family breathed a sigh of relief when she passed out of their lives.'

'They always thought her absurd,' Miranda agreed mournfully. 'My poor little Marcy! Silly in the extreme, I once overheard Grandmother Seymour say of her. However did she marry into such a family in the first place?'

George appeared to quiver all over, and Miranda realised he too was in shock. 'But, my darling, she was glorious!' he exclaimed. 'Jay simply snatched her up despite the family. She was like a flower, like springtime. Like you, in fact. What's more, she was madly in love with Jay.'

'Until death had to part them.' Even now Miranda couldn't cope with the loss of her father. She simply shut her mind on it as she was obliged to when her mother had flown off to America. 'To think both of them had to die in a senseless accident.'

George folded down an important letter. 'Both of them loved danger,' he pointed out dryly. 'There are other things I have to tell you.' He ambled to the huge plateglass window that looked out over the bustling city. 'The Seymours have been keeping you for the past few years.'

'What?' For an instant Miranda sat helplessly, then she moved towards George, her small oval face registering near-horror. 'Not *Blake*?'

'Who else, after all?' George shrugged his heavy, expensively clad shoulders. 'Marcy asked me to appeal to him, and I did. It was just after she financed that dreadful little movie her husband flopped in.'

'Do you mean to tell me Blake has been paying for my dresses?' Miranda looked down at her perfectly beautiful silk dress, humiliated beyond belief.

'I'm afraid so.'

'Oh, my God!' she moaned. 'I'd rather it had been an Arabian sheikh. *Anyone* but Blake!'

'But, m'dear, he's the present baron.' George sank down on to the big leather chesterfield. 'Don't feel so badly, darling girl. He can well afford it. The Seymours, as you know, are immensely wealthy. Why, Morning Star must be the biggest, richest privately owned pastoral company in this country. And that's not even the larger part of their interests. Blake's pretty heavily into mineral exploration. There was that enormous strike at Golden Mile. And there are other prospects. Positively brilliant, is Blake.'

'Oh, brilliant!' Miranda agreed bitterly. She was remembering the last time she had seen him. The way she had given him as much cheek as she dared. He was the most dreadful upper class dictator—and to think he had been *paying* for her; for her hair and her dresses, her university education and her dear little Porsche. 'Oh how I *hate* him!' she cried with a ring of passion.

'Don't shout, lovey!' George said perfunctorily. 'If he has interfered it's always been in your best interests. It was Blake who sided with you when you said you wanted to remain in Australia. He never considered your mother a good influence. Understandably, as it turned out. I shudder to think what might have happened when that gigolo finally noticed you had grown up.'

'So what's going to happen to me?' Miranda tottered back to the armchair.

'I rather think Blake will continue to take care of things,' George told her a little bleakly. Incredible to think that beautiful, frivolous little creature was gone.

'But I want nothing from Blake!' Miranda protested vehemently. 'He doesn't even like me.'

'Nonsense!' Far from agreeing, George used the tone of a man in receipt of privileged information. 'He may not have approved of certain things you've done, your current fiancé for one, but I assure you he does have a genuine regard for you. After all, you're some sort of cousins.'

Miranda's green eyes looked dazed. 'I'd better get a job,' she said. Gallant for a girl with no serious purpose in life.

'Not such a bad thing!' George murmured encouragingly. 'You did quite well at university.'

Miranda's head was starting to ache. This had to be a ghastly trick, a nightmare from which she had to wake. 'I'll have to speak to Shane.'

'If you *must*. . . .' George muttered when he didn't trust the fellow at all. A phone call to

Morning Star would reassure him.

When Shane came towards her in the restaurant, his amber eyes were glowing. 'Hmm, you smell delicious!' Stylishly he bent and kissed Miranda's cheek. 'Another new dress?'

'Yes.' Miranda gave a funny little laugh. Yesterday a rich girl. Tomorrow on the dole.

'Darling, what's wrong?' Shane took the chair opposite her, a very personable young man and well aware of it. 'Pining about Marcy?'

'She was my mother,' Miranda pointed out, somehow offended by his tone.

'Have you just discovered that?' Shane laughed indulgently. 'No one less like a mother I've ever met. Why, she behaved just like a perennial teen-ager.'

'She always lived for the moment, yes.' Miranda could feel herself becoming more and more upset. 'Whatever she was, I loved her.'

'Who wouldn't?' Shane commented dryly. 'She was the most generous of creatures. Everything you wanted, you got. Tremendous good fortune for a young girl.'

'But it's not like that after all.' Miranda's luminous eyes were still wide with shock. 'I can't accept it, but Marcy died penniless.'

The golden-skinned Shane came close to turning green. 'What are you saying?'

Miranda's lovely mouth quivered. 'I've just come from George. He tells me the money ran out years ago.'

'Hence all those extravagant clothes!' Shane's glittering eyes raced over Miranda's freshly sham-

pooed and blow-dried blonde curls, over the perfect
young face delicately made up with the finest cos-
metics, down the length of her model dress to her
beautiful, imported high-heeled sandals, the exact
colour of her dress. 'No one without money looks
like you.'

'Not Marcy's,' said Miranda, shivering in the air-
conditioning.

'Then whose?' Shane enquired so sharply he
turned a few heads.

At his tone Miranda's shivers gave up, and
something like anger flared into her huge eyes. 'I
didn't realise my money was so important to you.'

'Now wait, darling,' Shane leaned across and
took her hand—her left hand, so he could play
with the engagement ring. 'I'm simply perplexed,
that's all. And upset for you. Anything that affects
you affects me. How do you spend so much money
when you don't have it?'

'I've been kept,' Miranda explained. 'Just that.'

Shane's mouth fell open. 'What the devil are you
talking about?' Just for a moment he sounded
exactly like her mother.

'I daresay you have to know,' she answered. 'A
relative of mine has been footing all my bills.'

Shane kept gaping. 'Not Seymour? That cousin
of yours?'

'Yes,' said Miranda. 'I don't think I'll ever get
over it.' She sat there, staring sightlessly ahead of
her with no little wonder.

'And you just found out today?'

'Yes.' She suddenly leaned forward, speaking
urgently. 'Until we're married, I'll have to get a
job.'

'There's got to be *some* money.' Shane looked as if he wanted to shake her. 'Not even *your* mother could go through a fortune!'

'George wouldn't lie to me—and you must remember she had help.'

Shane was silent after that, his good-looking face marred by a dark frown.

'Okay,' he said finally, when they were having coffee. 'You'll have to approach this Seymour. Know what he's worth now? Millions. It's cruel really—one man to have all that money.'

Miranda shook her head. 'It has nothing to do with me.'

'Surely your mother still retained her shares in Morning Star?'

'George said no. When she married Clipper she sold up.'

'What a fool!' Shane said scathingly. 'Didn't she know shares like that are sacred?'

Miranda looked at him, smiling a little sadly. 'It was my money, wasn't it, Shane?'

'Darling, you've still got it.' Instantly the sharpness, the edginess eased out of Shane's tone. 'It wouldn't make much difference to Seymour to keep on supporting you. And if he's any kind of a cousin at all there would have to be a magnificent wedding present.'

'You don't know Blake,' she said gently. 'He's a hard man. More, he doesn't approve of you.'

Shane looked more alarmed than peeved. 'I beg your pardon?'

'Of course I've never spoken of it before.' Miranda's clear, pretty voice began to shake. 'But take my word for it.'

'But I've only met him once.' Shane didn't seem to be able to take it all in. 'He was quite affable in a high-handed, trained-for-kingship kind of way.'

'He didn't think you'd last.' Miranda emitted a jagged breath.

'Nonsense. We're perfectly happy together.'

'I know we are.' Miranda stared at him, confused. Weren't they happy? They always looked and acted as if they were. Shane was attractive, well educated, an up-and-coming young executive in an advertising firm, lots of fun. That was the thing that had initially attracted her to him—his easygoing, carefree ways. Hard, tough, dominating men were intolerable.

'There's a way out of this, darling,' Shane promised. 'I'm sure your dear cousin won't see you without a bean. I mean, you're an orphan.'

'Why don't we just get married?' Miranda ventured.

'I've *told* you, darling,' Shane shook his head. 'We agreed to get married when you turn twenty-one.'

'When I come into my money.'

'I love you, Miranda, for yourself.' Shane picked up her hand and lightly kissed it. 'I don't say you're as clever as lots of girls I know, but you're a darned sight prettier than the lot of them put together.'

'Actually I was considered a very good student,' Miranda said ironically.

'I mean in the ways of the world, darling. It's amazing how delightfully innocent you are. Quite unique.'

Miranda had no doubt as to that. Shane considered twenty-year-old virgins subnormal—a state of affairs he hadn't changed, for all his persistence.

'Drink up,' he said firmly. 'I have to be back at the office.'

That same afternoon Miranda drove over to see one of her old school friends, twelve months married and newly pregnant.

'Hi!'

They greeted one another with genuine affection, Miranda slipping an arm around Lucy's thickening waist.

'You *are* settling nicely into motherhood.'

'No morning sickness, nothing. It's blissful. I told Mark I could have worked for a few more months, but he wouldn't have it.'

'Men tend to make a lot of first pregnancies,' Miranda smiled. She herself had introduced Mark to Lucy and been rewarded with being chief bridesmaid.

'So what's new with you?' In the kitchen of their modest first home Lucy bustled about making coffee. 'I love your dress, but then you always look gorgeous.'

'There won't be too many more of them.'

Lucy paused in her task to look searchingly at her friend. Except of course that Miranda always looked wonderful, the small face was tragic. 'I don't like the sound of that,' she said.

'Put the coffee on, Lucy,' Miranda implored her. 'I have a splitting headache.'

'That's not like you, Mirry. You never complain.' Lucy hastened to plug in the percolator. It was not as though Miranda could be missing her mother. She never saw her.

'You're fond of me, aren't you, Lucy?' Miranda asked.

'Sure am,' Lucy smiled. 'Even if you were as plain as I am, you'd still draw people to you. You're so *nice*!'

'You've never cared I had a shocking lot of money.'

'It never spoilt you, pet.' Lucy cleared a place and sat down. 'Even the nuns in the convent said that.'

'Just as well, so I won't be so harshly punished.' Miranda stabbed her fingers into the short, silky curls above her right temple. 'The truth is, Lucy, as from a few years ago, I'm broke.'

Lucy's velvet brown eyes widened. 'I think you ought to explain.'

Miranda did, while Lucy sat quietly. 'Well, it's not so dreadful after all!' she said with a mixture of briskness and compassion. 'You're young and healthy, well educated. You could turn your hand to lots of things. You could model, but I suppose you wouldn't like that?'

'No.'

'What has Shane got to say?' Lucy's expressive voice had a strangely cynical quality.

'He was shocked.'

'I'm not surprised.' Lucy restrained herself from saying more.

'You've never liked him, have you, Lucy?'

A heavy flush swept Lucy's face. 'Oh, pet. . . .'

'You've never said anything, you or Mark, but I've always felt you suffered him for my sake.' Lucy pressed her lips tightly together, but Miranda smiled at her with a mixture of tenderness and coaxing. '*Why* don't you like him? He's good-looking, clever, lots of fun.'

Lucy's brown eyes flashed with anger. 'He's not good enough for you, Mirry. You're my friend and I love you. You were the only one who was kind to me when we first started boarding school. It never seemed to occur to the others that I was miserably unhappy, terrified of being away from my parents. You no sooner made a friend of me than all the bitchy remarks stopped. The prettiest, smartest, most popular girl in the school, my friend. Through the best and the worst of times. I've never wanted to hurt you, but we can't help thinking, Mark and I, that Shane is a con man on the make!'

'No!'

'There, I've hurt you.' Lucy flung herself onto a kitchen chair and burst into tears. 'Mark told me to keep my mouth shut.'

'I *asked* you,' Miranda pointed out.

'Dumb, dumb, dumb, that's what I am!' Lucy pounded the kitchen table.

'Now, now, don't you start giving yourself a hard time.' Miranda spoke firmly, used to the vagaries of Lucy's temperament. 'Anyway, the coffee's perked.'

'Are you sure you won't have some cheesecake?' Lucy looked up and blinked. 'I made it myself.'

'In that case I will.' Miranda hid her total lack of appetite. 'It must be a great pleasure to Mark having such a terrific little homemaker for a wife.'

'I guess it is.' Lucy tried to speak nonchalantly,

but the love and pride shone through her voice. 'Please forgive me for what I said.'

'I forgive you,' Miranda said quickly. 'In any case, I have a suspicion you're right.'

'Not that he doesn't love you.' Lucy looked confused and relieved. 'He'd be crazy if he didn't, but he's got those foxy eyes on the money.'

'Oh, hell, Lucy.' Miranda wanted to cry, but she couldn't. If she started, Lucy would really dissolve in floods.

'You told me yourself Blake didn't approve of him.'

'Blake disapproves of everything I consider fun,' shrugged Miranda.

'I'll never forget when you first took me to Morning Star, I couldn't take my eyes off him.' Lucy poured the coffee and sat down opposite her friend. 'He's the most fantastic man. I used to fall for him every vacation, but a man like that would never look at me.'

'In any case you've got Mark, who's not only very nice, but decent and kind.'

'And Blake isn't?' Lucy started to giggle. 'The thing is, Mirry, you're a little in love with him yourself.'

Nothing she could have said would have shocked Miranda more. 'Thanks a lot,' she said wryly.

'In some ways I'm uncanny,' said Lucy.

'I think you *are*, but not about Blake. I can't stand him.'

'And you know why? You're just scared of him, that's all.'

'I'm not scared.' Miranda was astounded. 'I'm not scared of anybody.'

'Then how come all your boy-friends, your two fiancés have been the opposite to Blake?'

'I guess because there's nobody like him in the whole damned world.'

'Don't get mad.' Lucy cut two generous slices of chocolate cheesecake. 'If you really wanted to work at it, you could get Blake. You have everything going for you. You're a beauty, you're smart, you've got lovely, easy manners. . . .'

'Lucy dear,' Miranda interrupted, 'you're wasting your time. I've never heard anything so unbelievable. Blake may be a very handsome man. . . .'

Sexy! Lucy underscored heavily.

'Even that,' Miranda acknowledged with a flash of irritation, 'but he's much too complicated for me—too formidable, too sophisticated. I don't like aggressively masculine men, the manner of command. I can't imagine how you thought I did.'

'There's something there,' Lucy observed detachedly. 'Some primitive chemistry, perhaps. He's not as immune to you as you think.'

'Haven't you grasped that I'm engaged?'

'Defensive tactics.' Lucy stared at her over her coffee cup. 'I remember how you were when Blake's plane was overdue.'

'How everyone was.' Even now Miranda's heart lurched in memory. If anything had happened to Blake that would have been the ultimate tragedy.

'You simple threw yourself at him when he arrived,' Lucy reminded her. 'And as I recall he coped beautifully with your hysterics.'

'He redeems himself occasionally,' Miranda was

forced to admit. 'Of course I care about him, but there are plenty of aspects of his personality I find terribly unlovable. Blake can be pretty awesome when he likes.'

'Not a man to twirl around your little finger,' Lucy supplied shrewdly. 'I'll admit I'm not surprised he's been supporting you.'

'Yes, isn't it awful?' Miranda's high cheekbones suddenly burned. 'Lucy, what am I going to *do*?'

Two days later a letter from Grandmother Seymour arrived, and Miranda's heart lifted a little as she took it through to the living room of her apartment to read it in peace and comfort. It had been an awful day—an unsuccessful job interview in the morning where her degree meant nothing and her lack of experience everything, an explosive meeting with Shane at lunchtime when she had walked out without eating a bite, and less than an hour ago at her second job interview she had been told she had too many qualifications for the job. Be that as it may, she desperately needed the money. She had made hefty inroads into her last cheque and what was left would run out before the end of the month. She would have to sell her luxury home unit, no difficulty there, and find a flat to rent. But then who did the unit really belong to? Blake? It was dreadful to be so beholden to a man a thousand miles away.

Grandmother Seymour's letter was like sunshine through winter rain. It sympathised with her again over the loss of her mother, though they were both always conscious of Grandmother Seymour's opinion of Marcy, and in the end invited Miranda

out to Morning Star on the kindly and diplomatic
pretext that Grandmother Seymour wanted to see
her. Not that they both weren't extremely fond of
each other, but Miranda knew well that the indomitable old lady had no time to be lonely. With
her daughter-in-law, Anne, remarried and living
with her politician husband in Canberra, Grandmother Seymour was the power behind the domestic affairs of a great station. Staff there were in
plenty, but only one Missus. Beautiful, bitchy Justine, Uncle Grant's wife, didn't count.

It would be the easy way to go. Grandmother
Seymour would never see her stuck. On the other
hand, it was about time she stood on her own two
feet. She had enjoyed herself for far too long. Pick-
ing up the evening paper, she turned quickly to the
positions vacant. . . . Not much hope for her there.
She sighed heavily. Ah, there was one. Ability to
converse with people at all levels. Plus the rub. A
high standard of typing. Food-drink waitress. Live-
in general help. Two children. *Widower?* She hadn't
even the experience for *that*.

Dallas came on at eight-thirty and she gave herself over to a bit of mindless enjoyment. No matter
how badly things went, life could never be as complicated as that. Anyway, something about the
pomp and the power reminded her of Morning
Star; the incredible aura that surrounded a family
that were unashamedly filthy rich. The only thing
different about Blake was, he didn't use his money
like a club. Or did he? Here we go again, she
thought.

Just as Sue-Ellen was going in again to see her
therapist, the doorbell rang.

'Drat it!' She knew quite well it would be Shane.

'Darling!' His amber eyes were penitent. 'You're not sulking?'

'Why not?' Actually she never did. 'It's been a rotten day.'

'May I come in?'

'Sure.' She stood away from the door. 'I'm watching *Dallas*.'

'Who isn't?' Shane retorted disagreeably. 'The rubbish people can swallow!'

'Beautiful people,' Miranda amended. 'We wouldn't watch it if they were all ugly.'

'I do hope you're going to turn it off,' he complained.

'As you like.' Sue-Ellen was on again, in a change of dress.

'Come here.' Shane was lounging back against the sofa, holding his hand out.

'All right,' Miranda said a little distantly.

'Don't you know how much I love you?' He drew Miranda against him and held her there. 'That our being together is all that matters?' He bent his head and kissed the side of her creamy, satiny neck. 'I know we'll find wonderful happiness together, if you'd only let yourself go.'

'You mean go to bed?' she asked bluntly.

'A lot of engaged couples do.'

'I know they do,' she sat immobile within his confining arm, 'but I'm just an old-fashioned girl.'

'You mean you're unreasonable,' Shane chided her. 'Or it's got something to do with being mixed up with the nuns.'

'How wonderful! Did you work that out all by yourself?'

'Some of it,' Shane confided. 'One of the boys told me you freeze when anyone comes on too strong.'

'It's such a price, though, isn't it, that a woman pays. I don't consider my body a trivial commodity.'

'But, darling, we're planning to be married. The way you act is unnatural.'

'Maybe it is,' she agreed with wry humour. 'You're certainly very attractive, but I've never felt as though I was in any danger of going overboard. Does passion really exist, or do we just read about it in books? Hope for it, long for it, but never really experience what the lady novelists would have us believe?'

'Miranda, my love, let me prove it.' Shane kissed her neck again, his whole body pulsing with excitement. It was like kissing a scented, tightly budded flower, tremendously thrilling. 'You're beautiful,' he breathed. 'Beautiful. Let me love you, Mirry. I *have* to!'

Slowly, very gently at first, he covered her mouth with his own, not really caring if he went totally out of control. He'd played Prince Charming long enough. What she really needed was a bit of manhandling.

For a few seconds Miranda had no thoughts at all. What was happening to her wasn't unpleasant. Shane, four years older than herself, was nevertheless an experienced lover. He was her fiancé. She should really be melting with desire, but she knew that she wasn't. Lucy had told her her wedding night had been the most beautiful experience of her life—perfect, the passion and the tenderness.

What *was* it she was experiencing now? Was she frigid after all? An unconscious revolt perhaps because poor little Marcy had gloried in love affairs? Certainly she shouldn't have been psycho-analysing herself.

Shane's hand slipped down the neck of her jade silk kimono, pushing the folds aside.

'Don't,' she said instantly. She had never allowed him any intimacies outside kissing.

'Relax, baby. I'm only going to stroke your breasts.'

Was there anything so terrible about that? She wasn't, after all, a prude. Her bikini was as brief as anyone else's on the beach. She had beautiful breasts, small and high and firm. Once Blake's arm had brushed against her breasts when he was letting her out of the Land Rover and her mouth had gone dry with fright. That was on her last trip, when she had already been engaged once.

'Oh God, Mirry,' Shane's voice sounded agonised. 'Don't you know what you do to me? Aren't you feeling anything at all?'

The empty spaces in her mind were now occupied with a confusion of sensations. The excitement was running high in Shane, she could feel it. If she allowed him to continue it would run higher, yet somehow she didn't pull away. There was a deep hunger in her somewhere, a well-spring of passion that demanded a certain touch.

Shane's hand had sunk lower, urgently seeking the erect, rosy nipple. Unhampered by the silk kimono, he had free access to the upper part of her body, the wonderful, feminine construction. He had made love to numerous girls, but none of them moved him like this exquisite little virgin.

As he roughly caressed her nipple she gasped, sounding very young and breathless. 'Oh, *don't*, Shane!'

'Hush, darling,' he muttered against her glowing porcelain skin. She was small, but so perfectly formed. If he only had her naked he could storm all her silly defences.

'I don't like this,' Miranda said a little desperately. Though it should have been beautiful, something was repelling her. Instead of ecstasy, a kind of attack.

'Just relax,' Shane told her harshly, clutching the rolled collar of the kimono and trying to pull it right off.

'*Stop* it!' She loathed him now. It wasn't romantic at all.

'Sometimes one has to make the decision for little girls.'

She strained away from him then, for the first time aware of his superior strength, the grim determination on his face. He didn't look attractive at all, but mean and purposeful.

'If you touch me,' she said urgently, 'I'll scream.'

'You're going to love it. I don't mind a bit if you want to struggle.'

'You can't love me at all,' she protested.

'What do you think people do when they get married?' For a second he looked furiously angry and insulted.

'Well, that's what's worrying me,' she said frantically. 'I can't think I *want* you.'

'You've enjoyed my kisses up until now.'

'They've never been so ... greedy,' she pointed out.

'That's your fault,' Shane said thickly. 'The sight of you. You don't know one damn thing about anything. It's unbelievable in this day and age.'

'Please let's stop now,' she said shakily. 'I'm sorry, Shane. I don't really understand why I'm so reluctant, but I am. Probably I don't love you at all, never did. I don't know anything—you're right.'

'Does this mean you want out?' he muttered through clenched teeth.

'I'm sorry.' She lay back helplessly because he still held her.

'I should have known,' he said viciously. 'You've been leading quite a few guys a little dance.'

'None of them ever turned ugly or unpleasant. Some of them are even prepared to wait!'

'Too bad you decided to make a fool of me.' He couldn't stop looking at her, the young, forbidden freshness. 'Maybe you don't care too much about lovemaking, but I sure as hell do.'

He fastened his hand on her kimono and pulled violently, and as he did so Miranda slapped him hard.

It seemed to have no effect at all but to make him go wild. He jerked her to him, crushing her, his mouth grinding down so heavily on hers she felt an uprush of nausea. It was terrible to be devoured. She really was a perfect moron. Fancy planning a future life with Shane! He wasn't at all what she wanted, and she cringed from this scene, like somebody else's nightmare.

When he picked her up to carry her through to

the bedroom, bruised and still struggling for her virtue, Miranda screamed—a piercing mixture of terror, misery and embarrassment. Other people kept their love affairs quiet, on the other hand she couldn't otherwise ignore Shane and be raped.

'If you do that again, I'll hit you,' he said viciously.

This merely made her angry. 'You uncivilised *ape*!' She couldn't bring herself to score him with her nails, it was all so vulgar, but she set her mouth to scream again. After all, most women were obliged to.

'Bitch!' Shane muttered, crushing her arms so she could only thrash them feebly.

There was a commotion from outside the front door and as they both froze ludicrously, the door was blasted in and a tall, powerfully built man plunged in, only marginally less frightening than a monster.

'Of all the arrogance!' Shane burst out, startled, then, animated now by recognition, gave a visible shudder. 'My God, it's you, Mr Seymour!'

This can't be happening, Miranda thought, trembling so violently she nearly tumbled out of Shane's slackened arms.

'*Put . . . her . . . down.*' The tone was barely above a whisper, but so deadly it bit into the brain.

Shane was alarmed and showed it. 'I assure you it's not as it seems.' By comparison with the other man he looked half grown.

Blake's eyes didn't even flicker towards the half naked Miranda, his lean body arched in such a way it created a terrifying impression of some big cat about to spring. 'I said, put her down.'

'Of course. Of course.' Shane hastened to do so. For the first time in his protected life he knew what it was like to actually fear another human being. Miranda had been nurtured by the Seymours, and Seymour looked mad enough to murder him. To the day he died Shane never wanted to recall these hysterical moments; the intolerable loss of face and the physical fear.

Tumbled on the couch now, Miranda was making frenzied efforts to cover her delicious nakedness, at the same time giving anguished little cries. How dreadful that Blake should catch them. *Blake* of all people! He had always thought her a fool, now he would think her a wanton. And he'd paid for everything. Even this little love nest. She moaned aloud.

'I must go home.' Shane announced. 'I really must.'

'Oh, you rat!' Miranda's small breasts rose and fell in bitter outrage. Her emerald eyes were glittering and her whole body was flushed with shame. What about when Blake turned his anger on her? It was obvious Shane didn't plan to be around.

'If you're wondering about that scream. . . .' Shane murmured, prepared to lie in his teeth to save his life.

'Shut up.' Blake took a step towards him and wisely Shane retreated. How did a man get such an aura of danger and destruction?

'She *is* my fiancée,' Shane suddenly thought to cry. He was pale and his amber eyes were black with fright.

'Fiancée no longer!' Blake's expression was pure detestation and contempt. 'She screamed because you were trying to force her.'

'No, *really*, Blake. . . .' Miranda had the monstrous notion that Blake might beat Shane to pulp.

'I'll hear from you in my own good time.' Blake swung his raven head, and at the look on his face Miranda fell back. Maybe she was going to get an old-fashioned paddling herself.

Behind them, the doorbell rang and Miss McMahon from next door peered into the tiny lobby. 'I say, what's all the to-do?'

'It's all right,' Blake moved immediately towards her, blocking her view of the living room. 'I'm Miranda's cousin, Blake Seymour, perhaps she's mentioned me?'

Just like a woman, Miss McMahon was smitten. 'Why, of course, Mr Seymour.' She took one step forward, staring up at his handsome, very definite face. 'I expect what I heard was a scream of joy?'

'Miranda's habit,' he said suavely. 'I never told her to expect me.'

'How marvellous!' Miss McMahon cried enthusiastically, overjoyed she had seen *that* Seymour at all. 'Is it really true you own a million acres?'

'Approximately.' Blake smiled at her, adding to her fantasy. 'Miranda is dressing. I'm taking her out to dinner.'

'Lucky girl!' Miss McMahon could see she had to be off. 'It's a great pleasure meeting you, Mr Seymour. By the way, I'm Heather McMahon.'

'Miranda has spoken of you.' Blake didn't lie. He escorted that lady to the door while behind the sofa Miranda crouched in embarrassment. At any rate Blake had got rid of poor old Heather. She was a nice old stick but an incurably sticky-beak.

Shane had disappeared into the kitchen, no doubt anxious to get home but unable to do so. There was only one exit and Blake was shutting that off now.

'At least you've got a caring neighbour,' he said now in a hard and disturbing tone. 'Come out from behind that sofa.'

Adroitly Miranda stood up. 'How did you know I was there?'

'The mirror, you little fool. I also happen to know you're as nimble as a cat.' He bypassed her and walked towards the kitchen.

'Listen, Blake.' Miranda flew to him, pulling down hard on his arm. 'I'm to blame for all this.'

'I know you are.'

'How?' she demanded angrily. It was one thing to try and save Shane's skin and another to be blamed when she was blameless.

'You're altogether too dumb for your own good.' His blue eyes flashed in his dark, formidable face.

What was it she felt for him, love, affection, hate? He maddened her so much she was nearly snorting. 'You never give me the benefit of the doubt, do you?'

'Who the hell would?' He looked down on her scathingly, the big eyes and the flushed cheeks and the flower and bird-illuminated jade silk kimono. Even now the deep V was plunging alarmingly, showing creamy curves and a shadowed cleft. 'I suppose you're going to tell me you just came out of the shower?'

'Believe it or not, I was just relaxing at home.' She pulled the robe together with shaky fingers.

'Which was why that delinquent pounced.'

'Don't hurt him, please,' Miranda said sharply.

'Only the brave deserve the fair.'

Inside the kitchen, Shane was sitting in a state of semi-shock. There were many things he wanted to say, but he couldn't say them for fear of instant reprisal. He couldn't even claim that Miranda had led him on. The only thing he could do was threaten legal action if Seymour hit him. Surely they wouldn't want any adverse publicity or to sully Miranda's name.

'Well?' He looked up to challenge Seymour with Miranda like an ornament on his arm, but somehow it came out sulkily.

'Miranda has just been pleading for you,' Seymour told him contemptuously.

'I thought she would.' What a mercy Miranda was such a kindhearted little thing. Abandoning the chair, Shane stood up. 'I take full responsibility for the whole situation. Miranda and I are deeply in love and just for a few moments I lost my head. I tried to hurry her, but it will never happen again.'

'Be sure of it,' Blake Seymour said, as arrogant as the very devil. 'Miranda recognises that she's made yet another mistake. She has no father, no mother. I'm her legal guardian. In the old days I might have had you whipped.'

Shane had the terrible feeling if they were on Morning Star he might have. God knows it was some kind of feudal kingdom.

'Give back the ring, Miranda.' Blake's sapphire eyes briefly touched Miranda's face.

'Maybe I've had second thoughts.' It was an

added indignity to let Blake have his way.

'What are you trying to do to us, anyway?' Shane, heartened by Miranda's attitude, somewhat timorously demanded.

'The ring, Miranda,' said Blake, without moving.

Miranda would have held on to it, only she thought she couldn't possibly endure any more of Shane. She dragged the diamond off her finger and held it out. 'I'm sorry, Shane.'

'I'm afraid that's not good enough,' Shane responded bitterly. 'There is such a thing as breach of promise.'

'*Is* there?' Miranda looked rather surprised.

'If you want to sue,' said Blake, 'go ahead.'

'You've kept Miranda so much under your thumb she can't think for herself.'

'Then I don't know why you want her,' Blake answered with his cool arrogance. 'She's got no common sense—and she hasn't got any money.'

Shane's eyes flickered as he took that in. 'She must have, as a Seymour.'

'A minor Seymour at most.' Blake smiled unpleasantly. 'I'm sorry, but the money has run out. Didn't Miranda tell you?'

'I couldn't care less if she had no inheritance at all,' Shane lied recklessly. 'I love her.'

'Ah yes, but does she love you? I can't help reminding you of the way she screamed.'

'She was frightened,' Shane said stiffly.

'Shouldn't that have altered your behaviour?'

In an instant the tension built up again and Miranda caught at Blake's arm. 'I'm willing to forgive Shane. Why aren't you?'

'You mean you want me to give him a pat on the back for trying?' Blake's lean face tautened with disgust.

'Oh, stop it, Blake,' she wailed. 'Just let him go.'

'You really don't want me, Mirry?' Shane asked in a bitterly disappointed, choking voice.

'Please forgive me, Shane, for not knowing my own mind,' she begged.

'You know, Miranda,' Blake said harshly, 'you're an idiot. He was trying to rape you.'

'I know that,' she said fiercely, her cheeks colouring hotly. 'It's not for that I'm apologising.'

'Thank God!' Blake clamped a hand on her delicate shoulder and turned her towards the door. 'We'll both of us see your ex-fiancé to the door.'

Shane wanted to shout and fling himself about, but he was still frightened. He was no match for Seymour in any way and most guys wouldn't be either. It was this thought that bore him across the room with his shoulders squared and his head thrown back. What it was to be a cattle baron, big and tough and miles out of the ordinary. He hated men like that. He hated Miranda.

Shane left.

At once Blake's company reached frightening new dimensions. Miranda moved uneasily back into the living room, feeling harassed and inadequate—in short, what she always felt in Blake's presence save for the reckless defiance. She had been too shamed for that.

'Where in the world did you spring from?' she cried. 'It's almost diabolical the way you always turn up at the wrong time.'

'Proud of yourself, are you?' he asked curtly.

'Fiancés come and go, and all because you have to have some man around.'

'That's not true!'

'If you ever thought twice about anything you'd know it is.' He looked at her disgustedly, a hard, formidable man. 'It's not funny having to save you from a fate worse than death.'

'What an archaic way to put it!'

'Especially on top of that scream,' he said witheringly. 'How you haven't got what you've been asking for I'll never know.'

'Sound judgment on my part,' she looked at him with a return of spirit. 'Only mad people do the kind of thing Shane was contemplating.'

'Do they really?' Blake raised his winged black brows. 'You're the one, baby, who's as mad as a hatter. You live in a dream world where there are absolutely no complications. Beautiful girls do everything in their power to turn a man on, then they screech bloody murder. Of course you and I know you're a good girl at heart, but how is a cheap opportunist like d'Arcy supposed to know? You come to the door with the most seductive thing you've got in your wardrobe, then expect him to sit opposite you like a vicar with thick glasses.'

'He's never been difficult before.' Miranda stabbed a hand through her golden halo of curls. Stress was making her act in a totally unsophisticated fashion. 'What's wrong with me, Blake—am I sexless?'

'What the hell is *that* supposed to mean?' Rather wearily he loosened his collar and tie, looking very elegant and elitist in his fine, expensive clothes.

'What's wrong with my body?' she asked. 'I don't react.'

'Little darling,' he said acidly, '*should* you?'

'Answer me, Blake,' she pleaded. 'I'm worried.'

He looked and sounded unbearably irritated. 'I'm sure when you meet the right man, you'll react.'

'I'm twenty,' she pointed out.

'So?' He swung on her so snappishly she was disconcerted. 'God forbid you should die an old maid.'

'Don't be angry with me, Blake,' she begged, 'You're always angry with me of late.'

'You know perfectly well why. I'm browned off with what you're doing with your life. You're not a carbon copy of Marcy.'

'I can't be,' Miranda said mournfully. 'Marcy referred to herself as a passionate woman.'

'But otherwise as silly as an irresponsible schoolgirl. You may have inherited her looks, but you have *not* inherited her temperament. There's good Seymour blood in you somewhere, a Seymour brain.'

'Then why do you take me for a fool?' She lifted her shining head.

'You act like one, I'm afraid.' His sapphire eyes rested briefly on her hair and her face, then slid down the length of the silk kimono. 'Where am I supposed to pin the blame, on you, or your latest boy-friend? Why don't you go away and get dressed?'

'Do you really intend to take me to dinner?' she asked with heightened colour.

'Heather will hold me to that.'

'She's really very nice,' Miranda said earnestly.

'I bet she thinks *you* have a good time.'

Miranda moved fretfully at the familiar mockery. 'Have you come to take me back to Morning Star?'

'Don't knock it,' Blake said crisply. 'It's the only damned place you behave.'

CHAPTER TWO

THEY were flying high over the back country before Blake told her he intended to set down on Kanimbla.

'For how long?' Miranda felt faintly appalled.

'An hour or so. The annual rodeo comes up in June and Angus is on the board of directors.'

'I suppose dear Val will enter all the ladies' events?'

'Naturally.' Blake didn't even look at her. 'Val's a superb rider.'

'And she so looks the part.' Miranda couldn't suppress a spurt of near-jealousy. It wasn't at all clear to her why she was jealous, but she was. Blake did so admire Valerie.

'How about letting me have a go this time?' she asked belligerently.

'You'd break all your little chicken bones.'

'What about the barrel racing? I'd be good at that!'

'The only thing *you'd* be good at is adding a touch of glamour.'

'Gosh, you're unpleasant!' Miranda fixed her eyes on the Aerostar panel. It was her first trip in Blake's magnificent new twin and she had already been severely reprimanded for calling it 'a quarter of a million ego-trip'. Blake had devoted a full five minutes to justifying its role and the reasonable price for excellence and performance.

'I'm sorry,' he drawled. 'Have I kept you short of money?'

'Don't worry,' she said violently, 'I have no intention of living off you for the rest of my life.'

'Good girl,' he said approvingly. 'You owe it to yourself to get out and do something useful.'

'Pig!' Miranda gritted her teeth.

'Because I happened to point out you're terrified of work.'

'I am *not*!' Her emerald eyes bore down on him. 'I had two interviews for jobs yesterday.'

'And they went off all right?' His sidelong glance was disparaging.

'Neither of them were what I wanted.'

'I'll bet,' he said dryly. 'No ten o'clock start and a three-hour lunch break.'

'Here we go again,' she said unhappily. 'Being with you is like being on a battlefield.'

'You're such a sensitive little thing.'

Miranda didn't reply. She sat brooding quietly until they descended over Kanimbla Downs. Blake was handling the new aircraft with exceptional efficiency, so she just tilted her head back while he landed the valuable beast.

Valerie was waiting; a tall, handsome brunette dressed in khaki pants and a crisp cotton shirt. She had been waving energetically since they had started the taxi-in, a bright smile on her full-lipped mouth.

'There's your girl-friend,' Miranda said laconically.

'It's early days yet.'

'Sure, it must be twenty-five years.'

'True love takes time to grow,' Blake returned blandly. 'Falling in and out of engagements would give me the shakes.'

Everything he said seemed to isolate her. Valerie was now alongside and from the sharpened expression on her face it was immediately apparent Blake had not told her he had his usual troublesome passenger. To compensate, Miranda smiled brilliantly and gave an exaggerated little wave.

Drat Valerie! There was no doubt she cut an attractive figure. More interesting, she was heiress to one hundred and thirty thousand acres.

It was very quiet now the powerful engines had stopped.

'Come on,' Blake said briskly, while Miranda fumbled with the catch on the safety harness. She detested men who demanded speed.

'Oh, dry up!' There was some satisfaction in knowing she was the only person who would ever dare to say that to Blake. Of course she was too small to hit.

With the pilot's seat slid well forward, there was a wide entry corridor into the passenger cabin, but as usual, he went before her.

'Couldn't you have worn something less trendy,' he remarked suddenly.

She looked down at herself, startled. 'What's wrong with this?'

'You must admit there isn't a lot of it.'

'Ho, ho, who's the worldly one?' It was a terrific little outfit she was wearing—bright yellow crêpe-de-chine pants, light as a whisper, with a matching little halter-necked top. In her view, perfect. 'I wonder if Boz is about?' she asked impishly.

'Is that why you wore it?' Blake was opening the big barnlike door, the lower half housing a small air-stair step.

'He worships me.' Miranda looked at him through veiled, seductive eyes.

'The more fool he!' Blake grimaced at Kanimbla's foreman's hopeless stupidity.

'Blake!' Valerie spoke up in her extraordinarily penetrating voice.

'Hi, Val.' He smiled down at her, a lazy smile, but it drove a flush out on to poor Val's cheeks.

'Miranda. What brings you here?'

Miranda was conscious of the hidden hostility in Valerie's fine dark eyes. 'I never like to be separated from Blake for long.'

Valerie didn't like it, the tangible threat in Miranda's every visit. She wasn't a schoolgirl any more, but a female threat to be considered. Still, Valerie rallied. 'You're looking stunning,' she announced. 'More like your mother than ever.'

In view of Marcy's recent demise Valerie might have softened that declaration with the customary words of sympathy, but incredibly none were forthcoming.

It wasn't until lunchtime that the McLaughlins heard the sad news about Marcy at all.

'My dear, I'm *so* sorry.' Nice Angus took Miranda's small, pale hand enveloping it in his huge, seasoned leather paw, while his womenfolk murmured incoherently, their eyes indicating that they weren't in the least surprised.

'Gran wants Miranda to stay with us for a while,' Blake told them. 'She's very fond of our fluffy yellow chick.'

'Who wouldn't be!' Angus responded gallantly. 'Surely then, you're going to be with us for the rodeo?'

It was obvious a shadow had fallen across both the McLaughlin women's day, so kindhearted Miranda sought to put them out of their misery. 'But that's more than six weeks away!'

'You didn't think you were going home tomorrow?' Blake eyed her with a chilling glint.

'I expect she wants to go back to her fiancé.' Mrs McLaughlin, as like her daughter as two peas in a pod, approved of a short visit.

'Don't worry, she hasn't got one.' Blake's expression was sharply ironical.

'Not *again*!' Valerie's naturally red, full-lipped mouth fell open.

'That's one of Blake's tricks,' Miranda said forcefully, 'getting rid of my fiancés.'

Angus, the sandy giant, gave a great roar of laughter. 'It's a wonder you haven't given him a nervous breakdown!'

'You have to think kindly of someone to get *that*!'

'And you think he doesn't?' Angus's blue eyes were shrewd.

'He hasn't for years!'

As usual, Mrs McLaughlin decided, Miranda was getting far too much attention. 'What about another cup of tea? she asked Blake with a radiant smile. 'Then you must let Valerie show you the improvements we've made about the place. She cares so much for your opinion.'

'Where's Boz?' Miranda asked, for a little touch of devilment.

'You leave Boz alone,' Angus warned her. 'He's half over it now.'

'I only want to say hello.'

'Of course you do.' Angus smiled. 'All right, you little minx, while Blake and Val have a serious discussion, I'll take you over to see Boz. The only thing is, you'll get dust all over you. Sam Dooley's here to break in a few horses.'

'Perhaps it would be better if you stay here with me,' Mrs McLaughlin looked to her husband to stop encouraging the child, remembering now that he always did it.

'It's all right, Mrs McLaughlin,' Miranda said innocently. 'I'm not asthmatic or anything.'

Neither was she terrified of horses, more's the pity, Nell McLaughlin thought with a little flash of anger. It was awkward that Blake should have the responsibility for this child seductress. She was phenomenally pretty and unfortunately more astute than her mother. Nell hadn't cared for Marcy either.

Blake and Valerie went off together, compatible to the *n*'th degree, while Angus drove Miranda, a borrowed scarf around her blonde curls, down to the yards.

'Do you think they'll ever make a match of it?' Angus asked.

'Eventually,' Miranda said, after a moment's contemplation. 'I mean they have so much in common.'

'Darling child, what about romance!' Angus roared. 'Dear God, we're not talking about station matters. A man doesn't marry a woman because she's good at cutting cattle.'

'I think it's hard for Blake to admit he needs a woman at all,' Miranda gave Angus the full benefit of her informed opinion. 'Women have been shadowing his giant footsteps for years. He's thirty-four and he still hasn't decided.'

'Do you feel he loves my Valerie?' Angus persisted.

'He must.' Miranda was touched by Angus's fatherly concern. 'She's lasted much longer than the rest.'

Angus seemed only slightly comforted. 'If you ask me, I think my girl's got a problem. I have a great affection and respect for Blake, but I can't feel he's ever going to marry Valerie.'

'Don't stand helplessly by,' Miranda suggested. '*Ask* him!'

'*You* ask him.' Clearly Angus thought Miranda could pull off such a candid question.

'Would it upset you dreadfully if they didn't marry?' Miranda asked.

Angus hesitated, then nodded reluctantly. 'Yes, I suppose so. You know she broke with Jim Chadwick when she could have had Westbrook as well as this. Jim took it hard. He still hasn't shown an interest in anyone else. It was Nell who persuaded her if she hung in there she could have Blake. I know Blake doesn't need another property; on the other hand, he's an empire-builder like his great granddad. Val wouldn't be going to him poor.'

'Nothing to be ashamed of in that dowry!' Miranda was succumbing to being back in the wide open spaces. It was a flawless day, the worst of the heat over, her body swaying while they belted along the track. A flock of cockatoos soared above the trees like a white canopy and as far as the eye could see there was nothing but the vast Promised Land and mobs of fat, lazy cattle. 'Oh, I *love* this!' she said dreamily, lifting her slender arms to the dazzling blue sky.

'Then why do you stay in the city?' Angus asked.

'I'm no one out here,' Miranda answered him, at once soberly, 'and don't let me forget it.'

'You *are* someone,' Angus said gallantly. 'You're a real joy.'

'Nice Angus!' He had always been kind to her, and Miranda smiled at him affectionately. How come the nicest men married slightly bitchy women, or did they only become bitchy when they felt themselves endangered? Mrs McLaughlin had looked as if she would rather have tied the scarf around Miranda's neck than her hair.

What on earth was she worrying about? Blake might be obliged to come for her, or even show her a little kindness, but hadn't anyone noticed Blake regarded her as a pretty nitwit and very little else? Just imagine Blake looking at me, Miranda thought wildly. I couldn't take it. The emotion, the fright and the utter cosmic forces working against it rose to her throat. She could never, ever, handle a man like Blake. She was only little-league, peaceful people.

With the fuel crisis, the horse was coming back into his own. There were at least a dozen held in the breaking yards and Sam Dooley, small but athletic in his ten-gallon felt hat, bush shirt, jeans and stockman's elastic-sided boots, was approaching his latest problem. It was a big, high-mettled brumby and from the way it faced away it was obvious it had never known bridle, saddle or hobbles.

'Better let Sam know you're here.' Angus heaved himself out of the jeep. 'His language tends to be pretty colourful if he thinks there aren't any ladies around.'

Sam's offsider, a young part-aboriginal, had looked around and now Boz, too, suddenly registered that the boss wasn't alone. He took off his stetson and waved it wildly in the air.

'If it isn't little Mirry!' he cried.

She knew she shouldn't encourage him, but her face and her pretty manners gave her no choice.

'*Boz!*' She held out her hands.

'Wonderful, wonderful,' Boz was murmuring as he was coming. The yard was twenty-five feet across, but Boz made it in record time. Miranda was the prettiest girl he had ever seen in his life—a pretty baby, as desirable as all hell.

Of course he had to greet her very respectfully, part of the careful show a mere foreman had to put on when confronted by a Seymour. They were really Royalty.

'What are you doin' here?' The touch of her hand was sending electric volts through his strong, lean hand. Boz was still in his twenties, tall, rangy, a pleasure to look at and very efficient.

'Visiting,' Miranda said warmly.

'Blake can't do without your company?' Boz tried a little mockery.

'Never mind Blake. It's Grandmother Seymour who wants to see me. My mother died recently Boz.'

'She didn't!' Boz jumped back violently in his shock.

'She was killed in a hang-gliding accident.'

'My God!' In a tough and dangerous job even Boz was flabbergasted. 'I'm terribly sorry for you, honey. Your mother was a lovely lady.'

'She was, Boz.' The tears rose to Miranda's eyes. Marcy hadn't been a wonderfully good mother, but she had possessed a grace not normally given to more deserving women.

'Honey!' Boz's hazel gaze met Miranda's drowning emerald eyes. As she stood there with a scarf over her glittering golden curls the elegance of her delicate bone structure had Boz's pulse racing madly. 'If there's anything I can do.'

'I've got to sort myself out, Boz, but thanks.'

'What about that fiancé?' Boz asked a bit aggressively.

'He's gone,' Miranda said sadly. 'Blake never much cared for him.'

'Or the last guy either.'

'True.' Miranda blinked her tears away. 'It looks like I'll remain husbandless, with Blake around.'

'Mind you, he's got your best interests at heart,' Boz told her earnestly.

'Why has it always got to be so painful?' Miranda demanded wryly. 'Anyway, don't let's talk about Blake. What's been happening with you?'

'Come on, then, and listen.' Boz took her arm and directed her to the shade of a beautiful red mulga tree with its shining, glossy leaves. Torrential monsoonal rain over the top end had sent flood waters down through the Three Rivers, the

Georgina, Diamantina, Cooper, deluging the great flood plains and filling up the hundreds of water-bearing channels and gullies that ran in a great maze over the strongholds of the continent's cattle kings. Kanimbala was miraculously green and Miranda couldn't wait to see Morning Star's brilliance; the fantastic sight of mile upon mile of wildflowers. No one could forget such radiance. Such incomparable glory on the blood-red desert sand.

They sat under the shade of the tree the brown people called the minareechie while inside the yard the big bay brumby bucked and kicked out and ran wildly in circles. The caressing swear-words had turned to words more suitable for a young lady's ears, and from his perch on the fence, Angus looked back at the two young people sympathetically. A good boy was Boz, only this morning he had given him a raise, but there was no use his looking at little Miss Miranda. Angus was certain Blake had plans for her.

They were still talking, Miranda gurgling delightfully, when Blake and Valerie drove up beside them.

'Hi there, Mr Seymour.' In an instant Boz was on his feet, holding out a hand to Miranda to pull her up.

'Boz,' Blake smiled, moving as gracefully as a big black panther. 'What have you got in today?'

'Nothing much. Herded them up in the Hill Country.'

'You haven't got all day to sit about, Boz,' Valerie pointed out rather sharply.

'Everything's under control, Miss Valerie.' Boz was always patient with the boss's daughter's habitual arrogance. Once old Angus was gone it would be time to think of leaving, of moving on to another property, of maybe one day starting up his own herd. He couldn't afford to kick like a brumby now.

'You'd think they'd hate it the first time they take the bit in their mouths,' Miranda said wonderingly. She had long since decided it was best to ignore Valerie when she was on her power kick.

'Just like a baby's dummy,' Boz smiled. It was the horses in the next yard who were snorting and kicking up their heels. 'The really dangerous part comes next.'

'Poor horses!'

'Don't be ridiculous,' Valerie drawled deliberately. 'They have to be schooled like everyone else.'

'Then I'd rather not watch it.' Miranda frowned at the sight of the now rearing and falling brumby, a hobble chain fixed from its right front hoof to the left rear hoof. It was frighteningly strong, its body jerking in an agony of fear. Miranda loved horses and rode very stylishly, but she had never enjoyed these horse-breaking sessions, necessary as they undoubtedly were.

'It's time we went back anyway,' said Blake.

'So soon?' A flicker of deepest disappointment rippled across Valerie's tanned face.

'Gran will be expecting us.'

Valerie didn't dare argue that one. She had spent a good part of her life trying to ingratiate herself with the old lady. The old Tartar, she privately thought.

Twenty minutes later Blake and Miranda were

back in the Piper with the big engines rumbling away. Angus and Valerie were standing well clear, waving, and Miranda threw a kiss to Boz.

'Cheeky!' Blake observed, his sapphire eyes glinting.

'What's the point of being a woman if one can't act like one?' she said sweetly.

They started the taxi to the holding point, then Blake selected fifteen degrees of Fowlers for take-off and opened the taps. It was like soaring like a bird, flying right towards the golden eye of the sun.

'When I go back, I'm going to have flying lessons,' said Miranda.

'No, you're not!' Blake said grimly.

She stared at the hard male beauty of his profile. 'You know, Gran's right about you,' she said, 'you're over-protective.'

'Of you in particular. What are you, after all? Five feet three of thistledown.'

'No reason to take me for a perfect fool!'

'In any case, only the rich take flying lessons.'

'Then I'll find myself a rich man.'

'One can only pity him,' he shrugged.

'That's only your opinion!' Miranda massaged her temples under the silky curls. 'Of course Val flies. It's easy for her.'

'Valerie has a facility for handling machinery.'

'So far as I'm concerned, she's a real pain in the neck!'

'I shall block my ears to that.' A smile curved his sardonic mouth. 'Why so jealous of Val?'

'Jealous?' Miranda's creamy face grew pink with

indignation. 'Perhaps you could tell me why I'd be jealous of Val?'

'I will if you want me to,' he said smoothly. 'But you don't want me to.'

'I like to do my own thing,' Miranda murmured evasively.

'Let's hope you meet the right man before you ruin your young life.'

Miranda gave a rueful smile. 'If I do, I won't expose him to you.'

'You were singing a different song last night,' Blake drawled quite amicably.

'I didn't know Shane was planning a seduction scene!'

'Surely you set it up?'

'That's unforgivable!' She turned her head to look out over the wing. 'I didn't realise Shane was so terribly . . . *frenzied*.'

Blake gave a hard laugh. 'So you answered the door in a little bit of jade silk.'

'What's so terrible about that?' she asked, sounding incensed.

He glanced briefly at her, deciding she was serious. 'Haven't you heard of leading men on?'

'It never crossed my mind.'

'Honestly?'

'Absolutely.' She gave him a long, hurt look. 'I'm not a siren, Blake.'

'Heavens, no, not at all. Not purposely.'

'Your wit's killing me!' she said dryly.

'I'm sorry.'

Of course he wasn't sorry at all. Needling her was almost a religion with Blake. She settled herself more comfortably into the seat and closed her eyes.

Gosh, she was tired! There had been very little sleep for her last night since Blake pointed out that he was so very tall he would have to take the bed while she made do on the sofa. Rather a comfortable sofa, in fact, but she had found it extremely difficult to sleep. To begin with, she had never been so close to Blake in her life. She had finally fallen off to sleep trying to think why it shocked her. A lot of women got hung up on Blake, but she was family. *Was* she? It was high time she sorted herself out.

When Blake spoke to her she jumped. 'W—what?'

'I hope I didn't wake you?' he laughed.

'It's all right. I was only dozing.'

'Darling, you were fast asleep. Wasn't the sofa comfortable?'

'I should never have let you talk me into it.'

'I would gladly have shared the bed with you. What's one little kid?'

Miranda was greatly agitated, though she knew he was fooling. There was an unnameable something that always flustered her about Blake. 'Oh, we're on Morning Star!' she said, in a wondering little voice.

'To the horizon.' His blue eyes were a jewelled flash in his dark face.

Miranda stared thoughtfully down at the vast, uninhabited landscape. 'I wish I had some great purpose in my life like you. There's got to be something more to life than having fun and looking pretty.'

'I'll go along with that.' His sidelong glance was definitely mocking. 'You're enough of Jay's daughter to sort yourself out.'

'But how extraordinary!' Miranda's eyebrows rose. 'I was just thinking the same thing myself. Sorting myself out, I mean.'

'At least you've found the right place.'

'I don't mean for *you* to take care of me. . . .' she turned on him quickly, then flushed under his penetrating gaze.

'You want to make a fresh start?'

'Help me, Blake,' she pleaded. 'I find it so difficult to talk to you, to communicate.'

'You mean since you became a woman,' he observed deliberately. 'I couldn't shut you up as a child.'

'You were so wonderful to me then,' she lamented. 'So terribly, terribly special. So kind. I can scarcely believe it.'

'But then you were a magical child. I had high hopes for you at one time.'

'Oh, shut up!' She moved fretfully, knowing he still shone for her. She could never find words for what Blake really meant to her. She ached for his kindness, yet he seemed to use his power over her to hurt her. 'Why is it the people we care about forget to be kind as soon as we grow up?' she asked plaintively.

'You mean you care about me?' His beautiful mouth curved in a smile.

'I do so want to. Really I think I worship you.'

'That's why you keep getting engaged all the time.'

She deserved that, she knew.

The undercarriage went down and Miranda sat upright feeling the same old thrill of excitement. No matter how many times she came back to

Morning Star she always felt the same; innocent
and free and enormously radiant. She thought it
had something to do with the halcyon days of her
early childhood.

Prolonged acquaintance with the Aerostar had
proved Blake's point many times over. It was like
riding in a Rolls-Royce, the comfort and the quiet-
ness. She could pick out all the familiar landmarks;
Blue Lady Lagoon where she loved to swim, the
Place of the Dawn Wind, where they often camped,
Chanangra, stopping place of the Great Rainbow
Snake, Kalka, the sacred flat-topped mesa guard-
ing Morning Star, over which coasted eagles and
falcons and always for some reason, a white flag of
cloud.

She enjoyed the flight in tremendously. Morning
Star really had to be seen from the air to appreciate
its size and its utter remoteness. Now the endless
flats were blanketed with wildflowers, a fantastic,
living canvas of colour, and every creek, lagoon
and gully ran silver with lifegiving water.

'I love to see it like this!' she cried. 'It's nothing
short of miraculous!'

'A barren waste or a garden,' Blake agreed. 'The
wild hibiscus is all over the spinifex country and
there are even ferns around the cave pools. Stuart
Radcliffe, the botanist, has asked can he stay for a
few days. He wants to take lots of photographs.'

'It's the incredible unexpectedness of it,'
Miranda said. 'It seems impossible such a display
of beauty could rise from the desert sands. The
paper daisies are blinding, and when you can see
endless miles of them. . . .'

'Hiding the lonely graves.'

'*Don't*, Blake,' Miranda said quickly, unwilling to let all the old tragedies fade her delight. Pioneers and explorers had died here, but right at that moment the savage beauty of the Inland was cloaked in glory.

The atmosphere was so brilliantly clear she could see everything in detail. Far away on their western border rose the remarkable phenomenon of the sand ridges, running parallel to one another like great frozen waves of the ancient inland sea. Between the ridges, perhaps a quarter of a mile apart, the troughs were covered in spinifex cushions and the six-feet-high hibiscus bushes, a sweep of silver, burnt gold and pink against the blood-red sand. Even the flat-topped hills and the hillsides were smothered in lilac lamb's tails and green pussy tails, waving their feathery plumes.

'I can't wait to saddle up one of the horses,' said Miranda, pointing to the hill country as she spoke.

'You'll wait until I can come with you,' Blake told her rather curtly.

'It wasn't *my* fault. . . .' She began to apologise for her last misadventure.

'It never is.'

Ahead of them the all-weather runway ran out like a ribbon. Beyond the outlying satellite buildings, then in its incongruous majesty, the homestead, the Colonial equivalent of an Englishman's castle and the seat of the landed aristocracy in Australia.

'Home to Morning Star!' Miranda sighed gently. 'No matter what happens it's always here.'

'Remember it,' Blake told her.

The Piper touched down like a feather despite a

brisk crosswind and as they taxied towards the
hangar station staff emerged from their shelter into
the brilliant sunlight—Kenny Harman, Blake's
overseer, Chilla, the foreman, Wally Eaglehawk,
their top aboriginal stockman, and arriving in a
station jeep, Uncle Grant Seymour, younger
brother to Blake's father.

'Looks as if they're all here,' Miranda offered,
then added a little brusquely, 'All except Justine.'
She had tried her best to accept Justine, but she
couldn't. Justine's manner had rather a lot to do
with it, plus the fact that Justine was lamentably
fond of Blake. Miranda found it outrageous and
she fancied Grandmother Seymour did too. To
make things worse there was little Andrea, four
years old and running scared of her own mother.
Justine was beautiful; Andy was not. All the Seymours were intellectually gifted; Andrea was considered to be, by comparison, somewhat retarded—
a bitter blow for Justine, who had desperately
wanted a son. A handsome, clever, vital boy who
could take his place close to the throne.

CHAPTER THREE

WHEN Miranda saw Grandmother Seymour, she burst into tears.

'Welcome home, little girl.' The old lady patted her very gently, quite different from the crisp, formidable lady most people found.

'What an idiot I am to cry!' Once Grandmother Seymour had been tall, but now, at eighty, she was the same height as the petite Miranda.

'I don't know,' said Gran. 'I like it.'

'Justine!' Miranda's heart pounded as she encountered Justine's long, Egyptian stare. It was a curious thing, though most people tried to give an appearance of liking in the name of good manners, Justine never bothered. Except with Gran.

'How are you, Mirry?' she asked distantly, without requiring an answer.

'Where's my little pal?' Miranda looked about her for a small, stocky figure. 'I've brought something for her.'

'I don't know if you'll see her today,' Justine said severely. 'She bit Miss O'Reilly this morning, then screamed herself hoarse.'

'Poor little scrap!' Indomitable Gran shook her snow-white head helplessly.

'A trial.' Justine was gritting her small white teeth.

More like a prisoner inside herself, Miranda thought compassionately. She was certain Andrea was far more intelligent than anyone supposed. Something about the eyes—an awareness, even if there was no verbal response. Certainly the doctors had found nothing wrong with her, and she had been trotted from pillar to post.

Justine's exotic, too thin face was suddenly transformed and Miranda turned her head. Blake was coming through the fortress-like front door with its magnificent stained glass panels; shimmering purple and blue and green and bronze and the most beautiful rose-pink. He was carrying her luggage and Miranda thought stabbingly:

'My God, she's in love with him!'

'Good trip, Blake?' Justine was asking with an intensity that might overwise have been droll.

'No complaints.' He gave her no more than a fleeting nod. He set the luggage down at the bottom of the great stairway that curved off on two sides and went towards his grandmother, who was holding her face up for his kiss. 'Hi,' he said gently, and brushed the soft, dry cheek. 'Now Miranda's here, I hope you're going to give me a bit of peace.'

'Thank you, darling,' she said complacently. 'I take full advantage of your enormous strength.'

Justine stood stock still, watching this loving tableau; the man, the old lady, the young girl. 'What a lucky girl you are, Mirry,' she said in her light, brittle voice. 'Think of how much it cost to have Blake come for you.'

No one replied, and Gran squeezed Miranda's hand. 'Why didn't you bring that fiancé of yours? I said you might.'

'They've quarrelled,' Blake informed his grandmother smoothly.

'Are you sure *you* didn't send him packing?' Justine demanded of Blake.

'Ask Miranda.' He shrugged his wide shoulders.

'He hasn't changed a bit, has he?' Gran said dryly. 'In any case, Miranda doesn't look upset.'

'Then you're no longer engaged?' Justine asked Miranda with rather a fierce face.

'No.' Why was Justine so intense about everything?

'Remarkable.' Something about the tone conveyed what Justine thought about Miranda's intelligence. 'You must be very difficult to please, don't you agree, Blake?'

'At least she always likes them enough to give the ring back.' He looked faintly bored. 'Do you want to come out with me, Goldilocks?'

'You mean you'll let me?' Miranda turned with a quick movement.

'Tempting as the offer undoubtedly is, surely you should be keeping Gran company?' Justine challenged.

'Except I'm having a nap so I'll be fresh for dinner.' Gran stood slightly taller. 'Go with Blake by all means, Miranda. I'm *so* glad you've come.'

'In that case, I'll join you,' said Justine.

For a moment Miranda felt a distinct impulse to shout *No*! but Justine had already planted her narrow feet on the stairway, deciding the matter. 'The ride will do me good,' she announced.

'Well, that settles it!' Miranda murmured to Gran as soon as Justine had disappeared up the stairs to the left wing.

'Humour her, dear,' Gran implored. 'Justine is

an unhappy woman.'

For the rest of the afternoon Miranda tried very hard to steel herself to Justine's unfortunate manner. Justine had never liked her, but surely never so much as now? There were digs and barbs and glances that showed plainly that Justine, for one, wasn't pleased to see Miranda back on Morning Star.

Yet there were compensations. It was wonderful to be in the saddle again; in the company of these lean, suntanned, *enduring* people. Busy as they were, all the stations hands raised their hands in greeting to Miranda. Most of them had seen her grow up from a sunny-natured, golden-haired cherub to the young woman who always retraced her steps to the great station they all counted the best, the most rewarding place on earth.

In the branding yards, Blake dismounted to speak to the head stockman and as they watched him walk away with his peculiarly lithe and graceful tread, Justine spoke her thoughts.

'So you stopped over at Kanimbla?'

'Yes.' Beneath the broad brim of her gaucho hat Miranda's eyes were a deep, lucid green. She didn't offer any more but waited for Justine to go on speaking.

'I can't think what Blake sees in Valerie. She completely lacks style.'

'Do you think so?'

'Don't you?' Justine retaliated, her light brown eyes hidden behind Dior sunglasses.

'She looks very handsome when she's dressed up.'

'But ordinary,' Justine persisted. 'Her whole

conversation is confined to cattle.'

'She's got plenty of company,' Miranda said lightly. 'Frankly, I marvel at her expertise. She's the best horsewoman I've ever seen. Don't forget she won last year's big endurance race against all the men.'

'So she's brilliant. So she should be. She's been at it since before she could even stand on her legs.'

'What *is* it you can't accept?' Miranda asked quietly.

'Why she should make such a fool of herself over Blake.'

'*Is* she?' Miranda released the silky curls that were clinging to her nape.

'Indeed she is!' Justine exclaimed bitterly. 'She's far too unattractive and unfeminine to interest Blake. If you ask me, between mother and daughter, they've assessed Valerie's chances all wrongly. Blake has never encouraged her, I'm sure.'

'Why worry?' said Miranda, not maliciously but with a kind of sympathy. 'Blake can handle his own life.'

'He has to marry some time,' Justine pointed out. 'The station needs an heir. He's well aware of that.'

'All he has to do is decide,' Miranda said. 'There are plenty to choose from. Any of his old flames.'

'There's no one in particular he cares for,' Justine cried vehemently.

'You may be deluding yourself, Justine,' Miranda said quietly with the voice of reason. 'Just because *you* don't like Valerie it doesn't mean Blake doesn't. In many ways she's very suitable, and shared interests seem to make people happy.'

'How would *you* know?' Justine's thin face was tense and upset.

'What does Uncle Grant think?' Miranda asked.

'He tells me to mind my own business.'

'Sound advice.' Miranda looked up at a parrot that was perched in the red gum a few feet away. 'Let's forget about Valerie. What about you? You've lost weight, surely, since I've seen you last.'

'I'm not dieting, if that's what you mean,' Justine said abruptly. 'I've always been very slim, but I haven't always been married. I thought it was going to be wonderful, but it isn't.' Her eyes were still settled on Blake, moving through men and cattle.

'I'm sorry,' said Miranda. 'Maybe you need something to occupy you.' She had always thought that.

'I ride. I paint. I fly off whenever I want to.' Justine's finely cut lips twisted in a bitter grimace. 'I realise I'm not very effective on Morning Star.'

'Well, it's a man's world,' Miranda was forced to agree, 'but there's plenty you can do. Take over from Gran. She's wonderful, I know, but she's only a shadow of what she has been.'

Justine laughed. 'I'm glad I never saw her in her prime! When Grant first brought me here, I was almost afraid of her. To tell the truth I still am.'

'But she's the kindest, strongest, most completely unselfish woman I know!' Miranda looked at the woman who was Gran's daughter-in-law.

'She's also an old dragon.'

'*No!*' Miranda spoke so sharply she startled her sweet-tempered horse. 'Behind the starch is the kindest heart in the world. It's Gran who always managed to find time for me, Gran who always wrote, Gran who wants me here now.'

'So you're her little pet!' Justine said, rather sneeringly. 'No matter what silly situation you get yourself into, Gran gets you out.'

'Well, thank God for the Grans of this world!'

In the shade of a stand of coolibahs one of the men was putting the billy on, his fair skin protected by a battered slouch hat and a bushy red beard. He looked back at the two women quietly sitting their horses and said something to the young aboriginal, who loped like a dancer towards them.

'Youngfella Charlie, miss.' The boy swept his ten-gallon off his black curly head.

Miranda nodded, while Justine looked away. 'I hope you've come to offer us a cup of good old billy tea?'

'Sure, miss,' Youngfella Charlie grinned. 'Soon's it ready. G'day.'

'Coming?' Miranda moved her horse.

'No, thank you.' Justine's face behind the big glasses was tight. 'One would have to be pretty well dying of thirst to drink that billy tea!'

'You don't know what you're missing.' Miranda pushed at her gaucho hat so it fell down her back. 'If anything, it's a treat.'

Justine was unimpressed. 'I think I'll ride back,' she said tonelessly. 'The station takes up all of Blake's time.'

Miranda stared hard at her, but Justine didn't even notice. Her gaze had actually never shifted off Blake's tall, lean figure.

Here, Miranda thought, is trouble.

They dined, as always, in the formal dining room.

Gran liked it that way, though forty people could
have been seated comfortably at the table. Indeed
the room was vast, hung with splendid paintings
and ancestral portraits and lit with two magnificent
chandeliers. Miranda fixed her eyes on a portrait
of the Honourable John Tennant Seymour in its
heavy gilded frame. He looked very severe and
handsome and remarkably like Blake. He had come
to Australia looking for adventure and excitement
and stayed to found a cattle empire.

'There's only one way to learn, the hard way,'
Uncle Grant was saying. Try as hard as he did,
Grant Seymour, a good, sound man, could never
have run Morning Star. It took a hard, tough man
to do that, a man who could effortlessly command
respect and attention, establish control and hold it.
Uncle Grant was a fine man, but he didn't have all
the answers.

'Give him time, he'll find a place.' Blake sounded
faintly weary. 'Tomorrow we'll go up to the hill
country and bring in the strays. I want the branding muster over.'

'Well, Miranda,' Gran spoke from the head of
the table, 'how does it feel to be back again?'

'As though I've never been away.' Her voice
dropped very soft and sweetly into the sudden
silence. 'If you're going to go out tomorrow, Blake,
I'm going to go with you.'

'I've got too much to do to look after you.' He
looked at her across the gleaming table, the colour,
the shape of her, the flawless skin and the fine
bones.

'I can go, can't I, Uncle Grant?'

'Blake's the boss!' Grant, fifty and still looking

very lean and youthful, chuckled in his throat. 'I reckon you know to handle yourself.'

'Why ever would you want to go?' Justine asked aggressively. 'You'll be riding for miles in the heat.'

'I know the hill country.' Miranda wouldn't take no for an answer.

'It's spread right over with spinifiex and a lot of wild-eyed cattle.'

'Then we'll have a grand time.'

'No, we won't.' With his arrogant head thrown back, Blake looked down his straight nose at her. 'You'll have your day another time.'

'No good arguing with Blake, honey,' Uncle Grant smiled at her. 'You've done enough of that since you were about twelve years old.'

'I've also done a good bit of hard riding.'

'Really, Mirry,' Justine drawled contentedly, 'why push it? It's much too rough and fast for a woman.'

'Right, let's have coffee in the drawing room,' said Gran. 'You'll get your ride in, Miranda, before the hills are clean.'

I'll get my ride in tomorrow, Miranda thought. She could handle the chestnut all right and she wasn't a complete fool. It was three years now since she had taken that thundering spill. Blake had warned her about the colt, but in those days she had a lot more dash than she had now. Her headlong flight had given her a bad headache for a week.

Much later Uncle Grant stirred from his comfortable seat on the white, colonnaded porch and held out his hand to his wife. 'It's such a beautiful night, let's go for a walk.'

'If you like,' Justine agreed without interest or enthusiasm. Although Uncle Grant always spoke to his much younger wife with the utmost courtesy, she made little effort to respond in kind.

'They're a funny pair!' Miranda stared after them as they slowly disappeared.

'I'm sure I don't know what anyone sees in marriage.'

'Is it the difference in their ages?' Miranda perched herself on the balustrade and looked up at the stars. They were incredibly big and brilliant, sown thickly all over the black velvet sky.

'It's possible that has something to do with it,' said Blake. 'Don't upset yourself about it.'

'He's such a *nice* man, Uncle Grant,' Miranda sighed deeply. The wrong man for Justine. 'And what about poor little Andy?'

'I don't know what's the matter with Andrea,' Blake said. 'If she's not screaming, she's hiding. I think she's driving Miss O'Reilly up the wall.'

'And who hired *her*? Miranda asked.

'Justine,' said Blake. 'After all, she is the mother.'

'She seems a very capable woman,' Miranda said gloomily, 'but she's not exactly warm and friendly.'

'The wrong choice for a small child?' Blake got up and walked over to where Miranda was sitting rather precariously with one arm wound around a vine-wreathed pillar.

'I'm never here long enough to get to know Andrea,' Miranda said. 'I feel she's trying to *tell* me something.'

'I think you're the only one, outside Gran, who *can* get to her.' Blake was looking down at her, his brilliant eyes half closed like a cat's. 'Of course, you're little more than a child yourself.'

'Some don't see me that way,' she said a little wistfully. It was odd having Blake standing over her like that.

'Are you trying to remind me of that particularly distasteful incident last night?'

'No, not at all.' She blinked her heavy eyelashes. Blake always excited and upset her. He was so broad-shouldered and powerful-looking, so sickeningly, vividly masculine. It made her feel faint. 'I care about little Andy. I wish I could help her.'

'The first person to help her should be her mother,' Blake said rather curtly. 'Yet Justine can do nothing for the child.'

'Can she really believe Andrea is retarded?' Miranda's green eyes sparkled with a kind of anger.

'*I* don't.' Blake leant his two hands on the balustrade and looked out over the softly lit garden. 'She's an odd child, even a cold, unresponsive child, but I'm certain she's not only intelligent, but very bright. I've got no time to spend with her. When I get in, she's going to bed.'

'She spoke to me tonight,' Miranda said quietly. 'She said, Hello.'

'Poor little scrap!' Blake said, echoing Gran. 'I expect she's bewildered and frightened. Justine makes no secret of her disappointment and Grant seems frightened of his own child. It's a mess all round.'

Miranda pressed her shining head against the pillar, a yellow trumpet flower tickling her cheek.

'Let me come tomorrow,' she begged.

'You know the answer's no,' he said almost gently.

'You wouldn't say no to Valerie.' Her green eyes reproached him.

'You don't ride like Valerie.' He turned his raven head, studying her boldly. 'I've got no time for your antics this trip.'

'Then why did you let me come here?' She straightened so abruptly, she nearly lost her balance.

'Steady!' His lean hands pinned her narrow waist, and suddenly they were looking hard at each other—he superbly composed, she feeling the terrible heat of excitement. Blake was the same; why was she so different . . . *different*?

'I'm all right,' she said in a husky little voice that wasn't hers.

'Your entire body's leaping,' he flatly contradicted her.

'I thought I was going to fall.' She was still arrested by his gaze, wondering frantically, what's *wrong* with me? Blake had lifted her, held her, teased her, ever since she could remember. He was woven into her life, yet everything was strange.

'What are you thinking about?' His hands tightened, the long fingers splaying out so they almost touched her tilted breasts.

'If I tell you, you won't laugh?' She moistened her beautifully indented upper lip with the tip of her tongue.

'Try me,' he said dryly, his handsome face cool and casual.

'Sometimes I find it difficult to decide how much

family you are to me.'

'You mean you don't think I should make you tremble?'

'*Should* you?' she whispered, rather stunned by the feeling inside her.

'Does it feel good or bad?'

She swallowed dryly, knowing he was openly mocking her. 'It feels downright peculiar.'

'Well, you know what they say, self-knowledge is painful.' There was a curious expression, almost tender, on his infinitely assured face.

'I suppose I don't know all that much about men!'

'And you've lived through two engagements?'

'I like to do things properly.' Briefly Miranda closed her eyes so he wouldn't see the very real distress there. 'Let me go, Blake.'

'Why? You fit my hands perfectly.'

'You've got strong hands,' she whispered, 'but I'm afraid for them to touch me.'

'*God!*'

The muscles pulled in his carved jaw and for a frantic moment Miranda thought they were both going to step out of their lifelong roles; a completely impossible situation from which there would never be a returning. But then an imperative voice called out from the garden and Justine was walking up the steps in her scarlet high-heeled shoes, regarding them both with cold malignancy.

'Surely you're not trying to flirt with Blake, Mirry?'

'Not for the first time,' Blake returned coolly. 'That happened when she was still in her playpen.'

'Quite right!' Agitated as she was, Miranda

quickly followed Blake's lead. 'Flirting is an important stage in a girl's development.'

'And you were a *very* advanced child!' Justine assured her chillingly. 'It's a good thing Blake regards you as he does.'

'Like what?' Miranda enquired.

'A responsibility.' Now the colour was flooding into Justine's white face.

'What's happening? What's going on?' Gran walked on to the pillared porch, sensing the aggression in Justine's tall, thin form.

'Just talking over old times.' Blake dropped a hand on Miranda's shoulder. 'Miranda at two, at ten, with wild flowers in her hair.'

'What *good* times we had,' Gran said. 'How we laughed!'

'If you'll excuse me,' Justine stood for a moment looking at them all, then she rather stalked to the wide-open double doors, 'I'm going to bed.'

'Didn't Grant come back with you?' Gran asked.

Justine shook her sleek dark head vehemently. 'He's gone down to the stables to investigate something or other. Nothing crucial, I'm sure. Sometimes I think he prefers horses to me.'

'Don't be silly, dear.' Gran's voice was kind.

'Please, Gran,' Justine said testily. 'I'll say goodnight.'

'I wish Grant *would* pay Justine a little more attention,' Gran announced when Justine had gone.

'What exactly do you want him to do?' Blake settled his grandmother in a chair.

She gave him a piercing, upward glance. 'Would

you miss him if he took Justine on a long holiday?'

'A good deal,' said Blake. 'But we'd manage.'
Now his brilliant gaze was entirely focused on the
old lady. 'You know Grant won't want to go?'

'He might have to!' Gran reached out a hand to
Miranda as if for comfort. 'It would be good for
them both to get away for a little while. Justine
seems very deeply unhappy.'

'She has a husband, a child, no financial worries
whatever,' Blake told her.

'She's primarily a city girl!' Gran was in no way
eased by this statement. She was very quiet for a
moment, looking down at Miranda, who had
thrown herself on to a cushion at the old lady's
feet. 'You saw little Andrea tonight, Miranda. Do
you think you could help to look after her?'

'But of course, Gran!' Miranda looked up,
flowerlike in the soft, golden light. 'I think I
understand her a little.'

Gran looked sad and remote. 'She's not
retarded, you know. She's seen all the specialists.'

'Perhaps more would have been gained if Justine
and Grant had gone along as well,' Blake commented harshly. 'Neither of them are any help to
Andrea at all!'

'But, darling, they're so upset!' Gran sounded
desperate. 'It's not easy, you know. I've never
known such an unresponsive little child. I had the
feeling she was autistic, but she isn't. Remember
Miranda at the same age? Bubbling over with life
and happiness. There's no laughter in little Andrea.
Miss O'Reilly has told me, she's in despair.'

'You mean,' Blake said bluntly, 'she doesn't
want to stay?'

'She hasn't said that. Not yet.'

'It seems to me,' said Blake, 'she wasn't what we wanted.'

'She was very highly recommended,' Gran shook her immaculately arranged white head. 'Yet somehow she hasn't managed to get through to the child. None of us have. I don't understand.'

'Don't worry, Gran!' Miranda was hurt by the little grooves beside the old lady's mouth. 'Surprisingly enough I think she was pleased to see me tonight.'

'And why not?' Gran suddenly snatched Miranda's face and kissed it. 'You're as beautiful as an angel.'

'Hmm, I wouldn't care to look at Miss O'Reilly too long!' Blake turned quickly as his uncle moved into the circle of light at the bottom of the wide stairs. 'Everything all right?'

'Fine,' said Grant in his deep, kindly voice. 'Time for bed if we're going to have an early start in the morning.' He looked around, noticing his wife's absence. 'Justine gone up, has she?'

'Yes.' Gran answered for all of them, the sad expression on her face suddenly firming to purpose. 'Stay for a while, Grant. I want to have a word with you.'

Grant's tall, lean frame seemed to crumple. 'If you want me to take Justine away, Mother, it's no go. We're far too busy. And there's the rodeo coming up. I don't want to miss that, and even Justine seems pleased about it. Going away won't solve the problem.'

'Up, Miranda,' ordered Blake, putting his hand

down to Miranda, who was still sitting on the cushion.

'Goodnight, everyone.' Miranda went with him. Uncle Grant might be accepting one problem, but was he closing his eyes to another? Blake was everything his uncle, for all his quiet dignity, was not. It was so easy to be attracted to him, and Justine was a frustrated and unhappy woman. Was it any wonder she felt this terrible sense of disquiet?

CHAPTER FOUR

THE men left in the pre-dawn, and even then Miranda was awake. Of course she couldn't go and in a way she was desperately miserable about it, but she wanted to help Gran and little Andrea. Going on past results, she couldn't hope for much, but she was determined to do her best. In a way, though she wasn't sure why, she was slightly afraid of Miss O'Reilly, afraid of crossing her. However unattractive the woman was, she had obviously given satisfaction in her other positions. Was it fair to expect good looks along with all the necessary qualifications? It wasn't as though she was ugly, but her face and her manner Miranda thought less than amiable. She couldn't put it out of her mind that Andrea might have responded to a younger, more pleasant-looking nanny, like one of those lovely, sympathetic nannies on television.

There was no one in the breakfast room but Cook.

'Morning, Mrs M.!' So far as Miranda knew, no one called Morning Star's immensely efficient housekeeper anything else, except Cook.

'Came down early, did you?' Cook beamed at Miranda's reflection in the mirror of the Victorian sideboard. 'You look lovely.'

'You smell lovely,' Miranda said. 'Been baking bread?'

'I have. Cakes and scones as well. Now then,

what are you going to have?'

'The same as usual,' Miranda pulled out a chair. 'Fruit, cereal and wheatgerm, seeing you make me eat it—forget the boiled egg. Your lovely strong coffee and two pieces of toast.'

'I don't feel I can cope!' Mrs M. joked. In truth she was delighted to have Miranda there, particularly as she had heard Miranda's first wail.

'I wanted to ask you something,' Miranda said seriously, pushing at the silver centrepiece.

'Not that wretched Miss O'Reilly?' Cook hissed across the table.

'Don't you like her?' Miranda directed an anxious look towards the door.

'Don't worry, she's never down at this time!' Cook waved a hand dismissively. 'No, I don't like her, but I've never actually said that to anyone else but you. She's a pill, you know—*ugh*!'

'In what way?'

'Grim,' Cook muttered. 'She's been in this house six months and I've never heard her laugh once. Come to that, I've never even seen her smile. She'll talk if you say anything to her, otherwise she stays silent. There's no conversation, and she's the wrong person to have around that child. Of course she can handle her in that there aren't as many tantrums, but it seems to me Andrea has gone deeper into herself. If possible, she's even more withdrawn.'

'Gran has asked me to spend some time with her,' Miranda said.

'Well, you always do that!' Cook stood beside the circular table, twisting her hands. 'That one little person could give so much pain!' She sighed deeply. 'And there doesn't seem to be any explanation. I just know she's not retarded in any way. She's too emotional when something breaks down those walls. Once I was looking for the mixed spices in the kitchen and she went to the pantry and found them for me. I'm not even sure she didn't read the label. God knows she's got a room full of books. I believe she can read, but Miss O'Reilly rejected that at once. She said she was very, very slow and would remain so for a long time.'

'What she really needs,' Miranda said worriedly, 'is therapy. A course of therapy with a child psychologist. She's all locked up.'

'Can't you do it?' Cook asked. 'Everyone says you're clever—a university degree and everything!'

Miranda sighed heavily. 'I'm not qualified to help Andrea, Mrs M. I wish I were.'

'But you *can* help her.' Cook looked steadily into Miranda's green eyes. 'You're gentle and kind and you're just naturally understanding.'

'It would make me very happy if I could.'

'Just try, dear,' Cook advised. 'Just try.'

It was immediately apparent that Miss O'Reilly wasn't going to take kindly to any form of interference.

'Good morning, Miss Seymour,' she said shortly, when Miranda presented herself at the schoolroom.

'May I come in?'

'Certainly.' Miss O'Reilly withdrew her hand from the door.

'I've come to say hello to Andrea.' Miranda

wondered why Miss O'Reilly was so hostile. She disliked quarrelling and unpleasantness.

'Andrea is in one of her awkward moods this morning,' Miss O'Reilly announced. 'I've had to lock her in.'

'You've *what*?' Miranda felt a thrill of revulsion.

'As soon as she promises to be a good girl she can come out. I really haven't got the time to explain our latest little dispute, Miss Seymour, but you may take my word for it, Andrea has been very, very naughty.'

'I wish you wouldn't lock the door on her,' Miranda ventured. 'I can't think that's good for a child.'

'It's part of her training. She knows if she starts throwing things she must be punished. Besides, I've spoken to her mother. Ultimately Andrea will realise who's boss!'

Miranda walked to the adjoining door of the schoolroom. 'Is she in there?'

'I would ask you, Miss Seymour, not to interfere.'

Andrea's wellbeing was the most important factor here, not Miranda's rising temper. 'Believe me,' she said as pleasantly as she could, 'I wouldn't dream of interfering,'—lies—'it's just that I see so little of Andrea, I don't like to waste my opportunities. May I see her now?'

'In which case, Miss Seymour, you'll be undermining my authority.'

'Not at all. I simply want to see her. She's only four!'

'And tremendously difficult. No one can deny that.'

To Miranda's mind there was something terrible about the woman's rigid smile. 'But we're all trying to help her, aren't we?' she continued in her pleasant, but resolute tone. 'Moreover, I don't believe she should be locked in her room. I can't think it harmless.'

'Are you qualified to make a judgment?' Miss O'Reilly's plain, inexorable face flushed.

'I did study psychology at university. It's important to a child to feel free.'

'It's important that that child is not allowed to continue to be insolent and destructive.'

'Could a retarded child be insolent?' Miranda asked quickly.

'Oh, come now, they could be very cunning.'

'Andrea's not cunning,' Miranda said calmly, but inwardly very upset. 'I wish I understood her better, but I've never had the opportunity to be with her constantly. I *do* know children set great store by people's attitudes and facial expressions and tone of voice. We can all well afford to be kind and patient.'

'Are you teaching me my job, Miss Seymour?' Miss O'Reilly asked in a thin, accusing tone.

'You know I'm not,' Miranda tried to speak gently. 'It's only that I want to help.'

'You'll help best by allowing me to get on with my job,' the woman said with something like triumph. 'I have the training, the necessary qualifications, and I have the support of the child's mother.'

'Can't you call her Andrea?' Miranda asked, looking at the woman attentively. 'You keep calling her the *child*. She's a *person*!'

'I really think, Miss Seymour, you should go. Whether you see Andrea later on in the day depends solely on how the child behaves. Mrs Seymour has given me complete authority, and I would remind you of it.'

'I'll speak to her.' Miranda drew away from the locked door, certain Andrea was pressed to it at the other side. Surely Justine didn't go along with the sense of this? Children might often have to be sent to their rooms, but parental control should keep them there, not locked doors.

She had to wait another half hour before Justine made her leisurely way downstairs, and for once Miranda was pleased to see her.

'May I speak to you, Justine?'

'About what?' Today Justine looked very frail, mauve shadows under her eyes.

With such enthusiasm Miranda found it hard to go on. 'Andrea,' she replied with painstaking courtesy.

'I wish you wouldn't,' Justine sighed.

'Are you having breakfast?' Miranda turned away from the stairway.

'Just coffee.' Justine still clung to the banister. 'Could you possibly get some for me and bring it out to the porch?'

'Sure.' Miranda moved away, wondering not for the first time why Justine had had a child at all. Biologically she was fitted, but little trace of the maternal instinct was apparent in her manner.

The huge, superbly appointed kitchen was a buzz of conversation and laughter. Cook was there, and two of the aboriginal housegirls. Miranda paused for a moment to smile at them, then she spoke directly to the housekeeper.

'No breakfast for Miss Justine this morning, just coffee.'

There was a flash of disapproval in Cook's plump, contralto tone. 'The first meal of the day is most important. Black coffee for breakfast is sure to give you bad nerves.'

'If you say so, Mrs M.,' Miranda agreed diplomatically. 'Shall I stay while you make it? She's having it on the porch.'

'No, dear.' Cook looked at the broadly grinning girls. 'Minny here will bring it out, won't you, Minny?'

Minny gave an uncontrollable giggle.

'All right, I won't push you into the more arduous tasks. *You*, Mary.'

Afterwards shy and gentle little Mary set the tray down on the circular iron-lace table, gave a graceful little bob, then departed, awash with excitement. She was exactly fifteen and destined to rise high in the household.

'Well . . .?' Justine asked. 'Make it short, I don't feel very well this morning.'

Miranda bit back a quick retort—just as well. 'I've been speaking to Miss O'Reilly,' she confided.

'Regular old battleaxe!' Justine indicated that she wasn't blind.

'Then surely she's not the best person to be looking after Andrea?'

'The last two have been a slack lot. This old girl can make Andrea sit up and take notice.'

'Did you know she's locking Andrea in her room?' Miranda asked soberly.

'So that's how the little devil can't manage to get out?' A wry smile deepened the lines around Justine's moody mouth.

'I should think she'd hate it, Justine!' Miranda tried not to sound emotional, when she was feeling rather deeply.

'It might make her conform,' Justine said. 'Did you know that she broke Gran's big blue and white vase. The one that used to be in the hallway.'

'But that was Ming Dynasty!' Miranda exclaimed. 'Early fifteenth century.'

'It didn't take long to break!' Justine assumed a wearied-to-death expression. 'Gran never said a word.'

'She wouldn't.' How ghastly, Miranda thought. The Seymour collection of Oriental antiques was possibly the finest in the country and Gran's pride and joy; she adored porcelain.

'Even her father was disgusted with her.' Justine set her coffee cup down so jarringly Miranda looked at it quickly to ensure it wasn't broken. 'Of course Grant should never have married. He's a born bachelor.'

'He loves you.' *Did*, Miranda thought.

'And I, of course, succumbed to the thought of all that money,' Justine admitted sulkily. 'There are plenty of marriages like ours, all in the name of money.'

'That wasn't Uncle Grant's reason,' Miranda couldn't resist saying. 'He was head over heels in love with you.'

'And why not?' Justine looked thoroughly bored. 'I'm twenty years younger.'

Sixteen, Miranda amended to herself grimly.

'And I was incontestably beautiful when I married him.'

'You still are!' Miranda comforted her promptly.

'What good does it do me?' Justine cried. 'Grant would really rather have a horse for company, and I can't carry on with Blake.'

Much as you'd like to, Miranda thought. It was as well to keep any woman away from Blake.

'God, I'm *bored*!' Now that she had finished her coffee, Justine lit a cigarette when Miranda had somehow thought everyone had stopped smoking.

'I suppose you could get away on a shopping trip?' Miranda suggested. 'There'll be plenty of socialising when the rodeo's on.'

'Oh, yes!' Justine drawled sneeringly. 'All those horsey people about. Dear old Val looking incredibly masculine.'

This indicated a terrifying jealousy, for Valerie looked very well indeed in riding clothes.

'I'm looking forward to it,' Miranda said. 'Everyone is. You must admit we have a good time.'

'I suppose so,' Justine admitted with involuntary truth. 'At least they dress up on the last night.'

'Diamonds, the lot.' The place would be swarming with millionaires, all in their own aeroplanes. Had Justine forgotten? 'But to return to Andrea, do you really think there's any need to lock her in her room?'

'Leave well alone, Mirry,' Justine commanded. 'There's no need for you to put your two bits in.'

'Andrea is my cousin.'

'Twaddle,' Justine said rudely. 'Your father was Grant's cousin.'

'We're still cousins, whatever you may think. I'm sure no one ever locked a door on you, Justine, when you were a baby.'

'But then I was the perfect child!' Justine retorted through a haze of smoke. 'That's why it's killing me that Andy's such a little dolt. It's not just that she's so slow—and sometimes I suspect that she isn't—she's so *commonplace*. It nearly strains my credulity. I mean, I'm good-looking, my whole family is good-looking, and Grant is a very distinguished-looking man. She should be a real doll, yet she's a square little lump!'

There were times when Miranda felt like telling Justine what she thought of her and this was one, but the wish to help Andrea was stronger. 'Would you let me take her for walks and swims? Nothing regimented, just casual.'

'You're not very clever at looking after yourself,' Justine said bitchily.

'I'm very capable when the mood is on me,' Miranda retorted. 'I may display a' certain recklessness on a horse, but I drive well, I'm an excellent swimmer and I've got plenty of common sense. Andrea will be safe with me.'

'But we've employed Miss O'Reilly to look after her,' Justine pointed out obstructively. 'I'm sure you mean well, Mirry, but I don't share your confidence in yourself. Andrea needs a very firm hand, and you haven't got one.'

Should she take the problem to Gran? Gran was an old lady who had suffered a lot in her long life. She didn't want to worry Gran, deepen the groove marks of age and distress. There was nothing else for it; she had to see Blake. Uncle

Grant, a first-time father at forty-six, couldn't seem to come to grips with his parenthood either. Distressed and unhappy as he was about his little girl, he seemed to rely on the womenfolk and maybe miracles to rescue his child from her lost and groping world.

The stables complex was almost deserted except for two boys cleaning up the quadrangle and another inside the tack room.

' 'Mornin', miss.'

'Good morning, Curly.' Deliberately Miranda sounded very brisk and efficient. 'Could you saddle up the chestnut I had yesterday for me?'

Curly eyed her with the same deliberation. 'Sure, miss. Where ya goin'?'

'Oh, here and there!' She gave the time-honoured answer.

Curly didn't know just how far he should go. They all remembered how the colt had thrown her, just as they remembered how the boss had gone utterly berserk and torn strips off Jimmy, who had certainly deserved it. It was all extremely embarrassing and Curly didn't budge.

'You wouldn't be goin' out to the hill country, would ya, miss?'

'I haven't decided yet, Curly.'

'Ya not supposed to go there, miss. The boss 'ud go crazy!'

'I'm merely going for a ride, Curly.' Miranda gave the young stockman an entrancing smile. 'Now hunt up the chestnut.'

'I could go with ya,' Curly offered, like a potential bodyguard.

'I'm sure you've got duties here.'

'Very well, miss.' Curly resigned himself to the inevitable. 'In any case, you wouldn't get me into trouble with the boss.'

'Now what's that supposed to mean?' Miranda asked pointedly.

Curly reddened. 'Remember the row over the colt?'

'I told Mr Seymour it wasn't Jimmy's fault.'

'I'm afraid that wasn't good enough, miss!' Curly gave a nervous laugh. 'I've never seen the boss at boiling point 'fore or since. Jimmy shoulda tried to stop ya!'

'I suppose so.' Miranda still regretted her past transgressions, but she wasn't going to reproach herself for ever. 'It's different this time, Curly. I can handle the chestnut and I don't propose to get you into any trouble.'

Curly strode away manfully, even though he wasn't at all sure what Miss Miranda intended to do. She was a very unexpected young lady, but considering how well she rode, he considered she could not come to too much harm as long as she stayed away from the scene of the branding muster.

It was towards this scene that Miranda purposefully rode. She had no intention of getting in the men's way, but to stay on the verge of things; about as far away as she ever liked to be. Blake always affected this over-protective stand, treating her like the merest novice just because of a few spills in the past. To be perfectly frank, she thought of herself as dauntless, which Blake strangely interpreted as reckless. She could take her spills along with the rest of them. It might be perfectly permissible for

Valerie to risk her hide, so the pertinent question was: why should Blake be permitted to curtail her activities? She had an eye and instinct for horses. He had admitted that much, along with the fool-hardy.

The chestnut was a beautiful ride and when asked to gallop, went like the wind. It was breath-taking, crazy, exhilarating to be flying across the flats. The chestnut loved speed and Miranda adored it. It was magnificent to feel so wild and free, and she felt a rush of happiness that was never allowed her in her city life. The plain country was a flowering carpet and in the dry, thin air she could see for miles.

Morning Star, the magnificent! Her favourite place on earth. Her mother had found it lonely and isolated, too vast to come to terms with, but Miranda had been taken captive as a child. She loved the space and the silence, the mirage that threw up the most incredible illusions and when the time was ripe, like now, the great Inland bloomed. To the north, the south, the east and west, the wildflowers spread for miles.

Miranda reined in the chestnut and sat staring. Mile after mile, to the horizon, the flowers went on, a white and golden glory, vast patches of pink and mauve and the scarlet of the fire bush. Could anything be more remarkable than a desert garden? She didn't think so. However exquisite the great gardens of the world, they didn't extend to all points of the horizon. Why wasn't Andrea here to see such beauty, to learn about the miraculous desert flora? It would heal her and make her whole.

Miranda rode on, fired with zeal. Maybe in helping Andrea she would find herself. She couldn't continue to live the way she had, meandering in and out of meaningless relationships, gravitating towards men who were almost entirely the opposite of Blake. Who had said that? Lucy, of course, and Lucy always had been a very shrewd observer. She would write to her tonight, ask for all the news. Lucy was the kind of woman who was a friend for life.

Kalka, the ancient flat-topped mesa and a sacred site for corroborees, was a magnificent sight. Its great rock walls rose sheer from the plain, the midday sun glinting off the quartz. Now its rugged slopes and broken gorges were an undulating mass of feathery plumes, lilac-purple and green. Up there on the cliff face were caves, the worn smooth walls decorated with fishing, hunting and ceremonial scenes; a wide range of designs that symbolised sacred objects and ancestral beings. Professor Whitney had dealt with the Morning Star cave paintings in detail, although both he and Blake were of the opinion that there were more undiscovered sites on the giant station.

Rounding up all the strays and stragglers in the hill country was the toughest muster of the lot. On the vast plains the helicopter had taken the place of the old drovers, but men had to ride into the harsh country of the hills. Miranda picked a horse and cattle pad that led up to the series of flat-topped plateaux. As a child she had been amazed to find fossilised marine animals perfectly embedded in the ancient rocks and even more amazed to be told that the imprints of the mighty dinosaurs lay imprisoned in the mud of the prehistoric lakes. It was strange, compelling country; a land of heat, desert pyramids and silence, except at night when the native drums took over.

A wallaby darted out of its feathery cover and the chestnut showed her resentment in no uncertain manner.

'Steady, girl!' Miranda quietened the snorting plunging horse. 'There might be a few more of those about.'

It was wonderful to see the country in such splendour when the memory of drought was vividly imprinted on her mind. The chestnut, her fright over, was moving eagerly up the pad, and ten minutes later Miranda heard the distant sounds of men and dogs and cattle. The top of the bluff would be an excellent vantage point. She didn't plan to get in anyone's way, just talk to Blake. After all, there wasn't that much time. It had been terribly hard to walk away from Miss O'Reilly when she had felt like knocking down a door. In the past she had made some attempts to communicate her thoughts about little Andrea to Uncle Grant, but he had always either averted his eyes, changed the conversation or made a hasty retreat. There were many good, kind men in the world, but not all of them were meant to be fathers, just as Marcy had never been a responsible, aware parent. At least there had never been hostile feelings between them, which didn't seem to be the case with Andrea. She was distinctly unfriendly towards both her parents.

The sounds of the muster were stronger, reverberating bellows and barks. Close to her but unseen, screened by the eternal spinifex and the purple-flowering succulent, the parakeelya, a wounded dingo lay in wait. Only that morning it had attacked and pulled down a calf, and there it lay crouched, hostile to the presence of horse and rider. One rifle shot had missed it; it seemed like only a matter of time.

The wild dog made no noise at all. As Miranda rode past, it sprang with a powerful surge of its yellow body, intent on savaging her booted foot. To those that knew it, this huge wild dog was a calf-killer, with a history of attacks on the station dogs and even riding stockmen.

Taken completely unawares, Miranda did well to remain in the saddle. The chestnut reared and began wheeling in circles, screaming and snorting, while Miranda tried to fight the dingo off with no more than her felt hat.

'Get off, you brute!' she shouted, changing her tactics and weaving the chestnut this way and that. One of those plunging hoofs just could hit the dingo. It was her only chance. A fang had already pierced the leather of her riding boot. She was a good rider, but right then she had never been better, yelling encouragement to her horse and curses at the dingo. It kept at her in a fury, seemingly intent on pulling her out of the saddle.

A moment later there was a sound they all recognised—the furious bark of a cattle dog. It tore over the rocky ground, a big bluey, and the dingo gave a spine-chilling howl and wheeled to face the twenty-feet-distant dog.

It would be a fight to the death, Miranda was

sure, when all the stations dogs were valuable, trained to do a job well suited to them. The two dogs, wild and domestic, sprang at each other and met in mid-air, the air splintered and made ugly with the sounds of their slathering and growling.

It was all very terrifying, but as Miranda charged them in an effort to break the fight up, neither dog took the slightest notice of her but went for each other's throats. There was blood on both their bodies, flying fur.

Help from another direction came suddenly. A man on horseback was clearly outlined against the brilliant blue sky, sat his horse, took careful aim, then with crack marksmanship dropped the dingo in a matter of seconds. The savage assault was over, but the chestnut, thoroughly spooked, got in one almighty buck that sent Miranda, who had been staring uphill, flying into the spinifex cushions despite her immediate and instinctive backward move to keep her weight as much as possible off the front of her bucking, unbalanced horse.

She landed like a gymnast, unhurt but shaken, while the chestnut raced back along the pad, leaving a red trail of dust until it reached the flats.

'It beats me why you can't do what you're told!' Blake was leaning over her, blue eyes blazing.

'Okay, *okay*!' she snapped.

'Are you hurt?'

'Hurt enough.' She eased herself half up. 'I'm more interested in the bluey. How is he?'

'Pretty bloody.' Blake made no attempt to dilute the anger in his voice. 'What in sweet hell are you doing here?'

'Hoping to have a word with you.'

'Sit still,' he said in that tough, autocratic way of his. 'Your boot's punctured, did you know that?'

'Strangely I haven't felt a thing.'

'Let's see.' Astonishingly gently considering his intimidating mien, he drew off her riding boot, then the sock and got a hand on her foot.

'Oh, yuck!' Miranda stared incredulously at her bleeding foot.

'I hope you've had your tetanus booster.'

'I was meaning to,' she apologised, feeling always in the wrong.

'Dear God!' Blake gave rather a heartless shrug. 'You'll have to have one now.'

'I hate the sight of blood.' She mentioned this because she was feeling rather faint.

'Then don't look.' He bent over her, then picked her up like a feather. 'Honestly, Miranda, you amaze me inasmuch as you're the only damned person I know who totally ignores what I have to say. Why *is* that?'

'Why not? It would be perfectly horrible if you had all your own way.'

When she saw the cattle dog, Miranda felt a pang of horror. 'Oh, poor old fellow!' she said, sounding like she was about to cry. Why, the bluey had saved her!

'Do stop!' Blake looked down at her. 'The dog will be all right.'

'Oh, I *hope* so!' she wailed.

Blake eased her on to his beautiful black mare, who came at his signal, then turned to greet Kenny and Chilla, who had beaten world records to get there.

'Strewth!' Chilla was clearly upset at the sight of the dogs, sitting his stringy grey gelding and staring.

'Isn't that the —— we've been hunting?' Kenny asked, 'Beg your pardon, miss.' He walked briskly past Miranda, pondering over the big dingo's fallen body.

'It is.' Blake half turned towards him. 'Do what you can for Toby. I'm sure he'll be all right.'

'Yair!' Chilla, who trained the dogs, sounded convinced. 'Some shot!' he remarked fleetingly. Now his sun-creased blue eyes focused on Miranda, regarding her aghast. 'Ya ain't hurt, are ya, miss?'

She nodded and dragged in a whistling breath. 'I was lucky Toby was here to save me.'

'He's game, Toby!' Chilla told her cheerfully, while Toby responded with a thump of his tail. ' 'Course, if the boss hadn't arrived it might have been a calamity.'

'Yes.' Miranda dipped her blonde head inadequately. She would thank Blake later on. The blood was splashed in a scarlet stain down her small, pale foot.

Seconds later Blake thrust himself up into the saddle, drawing her back against him. 'Here I go again!' he exclaimed laconically, 'swallowing curls.'

'I don't know where my hat is.'

'A long way down,' Curly peered down the slopes.

'I'll take Miranda back,' Blake told Kenny, unnecessarily.

'Please don't bother.'

All three men ignored her. 'Don't worry, boss, I

can manage here.' Kenny stood back. 'The fact you
picked off that stinkin' dingo has lifted my spirits.
He had to be stopped—though I didn't reckon on
Miss Miranda bein' the one to do it.'

They wound down the twisty slopes, slewing
diagonally across the flower-strewn plains until
they came on the Seven-Mile Creek. The mare
moved through the thick grass, stepping delicately
between clumps of deliciously scented lilies.

'Let's clean that wound,' Blake said.

'Won't it wait until we get home?'

'No.' He frowned and shook his head.

Seven-Mile Creek was a splendid silver-green
stretch of crystal clear water and, in some places,
very deep. Blake dismounted swiftly and raised his
arms for Miranda.

'I never think I'm going to land in trouble,' she
said jerkily, fixing her eyes on a pearly button in
his denim shirt. Just riding up against him had
covered her body in a hot flush.

'Meanwhile it happens every time.' For a second
they were very close and Miranda had the shuddering feeling she might sway against him and stay
there. 'Miranda . . .?' he angled his dark head
sharply to look down into her eyes. 'What now?'

I'm frightened, Miranda thought. *Frightened.*
Oh God! She had known Blake all her life. Often
she had thought he was going to murder her, now
some wicked, black magic had reared its dangerous
head.

'Are you faint?' he asked quickly, his hand
suddenly biting into the soft skin at her waist.

'I don't think so,' she said appealingly. 'Don't
worry about me, I can hop down to the water.'

His fine white teeth actually snapped together. 'Never mind, you poor little soul—I shall carry you. It seems to be one of my roles in life.'

'At least I'm light enough not to make your back ache.'

The water was unexpectedly icy cold. 'Oh, it's *freezing*! I had no idea.'

He urged her rather curtly to sit down on a boulder and Miranda did so while he cleansed the wound. To combat the compulsive lunacy of her feelings—to stroke the polished bronze of his cheek, to sink her fingers in the crisp waves of his hair—she stared up at the emerald ring of trees. There was a black cockatoo high above their heads. The aborigines worshipped these birds and gathered the bright tail feathers for ceremonial performances.

'Is it still hurting?' Blake asked. His darkly tanned face looked serious and concerned.

'Mildly.' She thought the smarting in her foot of little interest compared to the thumping of her heart. Her whole body seemed to be vibrating. 'You're so good to me, Blake.'

'Don't I know it!' he retorted dryly.

'Isn't this a beautiful place!' she whispered fervently. 'Once upon a time, it must have been a sacred site.'

'Once upon a time, Miranda, you lived in the sea and you had a fish's tail.'

Something in his voice made her catch her breath. She was aware of everything, the sky and the water and the trees, the peace and the mystical power. Most of all she was aware of the man who held her small foot in his hand.

'You've got a funny idea about me.' She stared at him with a strange expression in her green eyes.

'Forgive me,' he said dryly. 'I haven't. You're a siren, Miranda. Yesterday, today and tomorrow.'

'And you're so immune?' Immediately she said it, she trembled. The words had simply tripped off her tongue; she had never meant to say them at all.

'Sweetheart, I know you like fascinating men.' He reached up and pulled one of the golden curls that rayed around her head.

'But that's all I like, Blake. I'm frigid, as opposed to the way I look.'

'Frigid?' he said in an amused, mocking voice.

'*Yes*, and two fiancés haven't changed that.'

'I pity you, darling.' He sounded completely unimpressed.

'If only you'd believe me,' she cried earnestly. 'I've only just discovered it in myself.'

'If anything I'm glad.' The tone was as baiting as the expression on his hard, handsome face. 'Next thing you're going to ask me to kiss you. I don't think you'll rest until I do.'

'You're crazy!' She put a protective hand up, alarmed.

'No, I'm honest, Miranda. You're not.'

The air was filled with the scent of lilies and there was true anxiety in her large green eyes. She realised now how foolishly she had spoken. Blake meant lots of things for her; strength, security, the whole pattern of her life. She was upset now, by the excitement, the frightful, dangerous, dazzling excitement. She did not want . . . did not want . . . there, she was ashamed of even thinking it.

Blake stood up suddenly, a certain tension behind his glittering blue eyes. 'Come on, my frigid beauty, I have to think seriously about getting you home.'

'Please.' She stretched out one hand to him, feeling now the most terrible pang of misery. Was it a woman's nature to be so madly perverse?

'You *are* easily frightened!' He swung her up in his arms.

'Don't you want to know why?'

'I know why,' he said coolly. 'It's all so damned obvious.'

In a flash she was angry. He was always so perfectly hateful! 'Are you suggesting I'm making . . . *overtures* to *you*?' she said explosively.

'My dear child, I know you are.'

'You're a brute, Blake!'

'If you like.' His blue eyes were a startling shock of colour. 'Anyway, little one, I'm prepared to treat the whole thing as a natural part of your development.'

'Don't play games with me, Blake,' she said wrathfully, 'I'm not dear old adoring Val. You're going to marry her, aren't you?'

'Are you asking or telling me?'

'You'd better put me down.'

'Sure,' he deposited her none too gently on the thick carpet of grass, then while her eyes widened, lowered his powerful, lean frame down beside her.

'Are we going to have a chat?' she asked acidly, her cameo face flushed and ardent.

'Certainly not! I'm going to do this thing right.'

'Oh, Blake——' she stared down at her bare foot.

'Afraid, baby?'

'Yes.'

'We must know if you're frigid or not.'

As he gazed back at her quickly, she saw the laughter and the mockery and burst out angrily: 'Oh, damn you . . . damn you. . . .'

The words lapsed into silence beneath his mouth. If Miranda lived a thousand years she would never forget that exact moment. Her whole body went forth to meet him; her soul. She opened her mouth passionately, fearing she might faint away before she had time to live this. God, how different kisses were! She had never been kissed before in her life, never felt the hard ecstasy of a man's mouth.

Just as he had her half mad, Blake released her, holding her down in the freshly scented grass. 'Frigid, indeed,' he said a little cruelly.

'I was wrong.' How could she say otherwise after that breathtaking response? 'It's all very simple, really. I've been kissing the wrong people.'

'And causing a few people a lot of grief. Poor old George—me. Gran has been in agonies wondering what was happening to you so far from home.'

'I can look after myself,' she exclaimed, looking up into his arrogant, beautifully sculptured face. His eyelashes were very thick, absolutely jetty around his deeply blue eyes. She had never seen exactly that depth of colour, so disturbing in such a particularly masculine man.

She stared back fascinated, while Blake seemed to be controlling a certain desire to punish her.

'I wouldn't boast about that!' he warned her with hard derision. 'In fact, I'm beginning to believe in the power of prayer. Gran sent me to get you and I certainly arrived in the nick of time.'

'Go on, rub it in!'

'I will.' The lines bracketing his mouth deepened sardonically. 'I remember it all in lurid detail. I haven't seen you with so few clothes on since you were three years old.'

'All right, so you didn't like what you saw!'

'I found it terribly unacceptable. In fact, I'm amazed you've emerged so innocent and uncorrupted. But then you're a surprising girl.'

There was no doubt as to that. Terrible visions of herself and Blake were unravelling Miranda's mind. Blake's mouth on hers, Blake's hands on her breasts. She couldn't allow herself to think about it, it was such an awful revelation. Just a brief glimpse of her own sexuality had shocked her, making her own diagnosis laughable to an extreme.

Frigid—how comical!

'Don't be angry with me, Blake,' she said in a soft, pleading tone. 'I hate it when you're angry with me.'

'So you do everything in your power to exasperate me, but that's by the way.'

She felt a little sad, because it was true. 'I promise I won't worry you or George or Gran from now on. I've seen the error of my ways.'

'That's obvious!' The mocking light flared in his brilliant blue eyes. 'Now you're going to have a little romance with me.'

'No—believe me. No! I'm the merest novice compared to you.'

'We can alter that.' He bent over her again.

'Don't, Blake.' She said it, though she was shaking with longing. Where could such madness lead?

'I thought you liked to scream yourself hoarse?'

Miranda had the feeling she was going to hear that for the rest of her life. 'You'll never forgive me, will you?'

'No.' His lean brown hands encircled her creamy throat. 'And there's not a goddamned thing you can do about it.'

CHAPTER FIVE

THE tetanus shot hurt like the devil.

'There, there,' Gran said comfortingly.

'I think you enjoyed that,' Miranda accused Blake.

'Darling, a doctor couldn't have done it better.'

'It must be five years since your last booster injection,' Gran estimated. 'Around a cattle station any wound, no matter how trivial, must be treated. If you'd ever seen a death from tetanus you wouldn't complain about an injection.'

'Have you, Gran?' Miranda asked the old lady.

'I have,' Gran said grimly. 'It's a terrible way to die.'

Miranda stared down at her bandaged foot. 'It's only a fairly small puncture.'

'And more dangerous than a surface abrasion.' Blake lifted her chin and looked at her. 'You're rather white.'

'Cook is making us a cup of tea.' Gran stared up at her tall, handsome grandson. 'You'll stay, won't you, darling?'

'For about ten minutes.' Blake was observing Miranda's troubled face. The flawless skin *was* too pale. 'You'll feel better in a few moments,' he said, towering over her as she sat on the table.

'I'll tell Cook.' Gran looked from one to the other. 'Don't worry, Blake. Her colour will come back in a minute or so. She's always been the same about injections.'

'That's true enough.' Blake leant back against the cabinet, hard and lean and superbly fit.

'There's something I have to talk to you about,' Miranda said plaintively when Gran had gone.

'Can't it wait?'

She shook her silky head.

'Well then?'

'It's about Andrea.' She looked up at him, her eyes huge and intense. 'Did you know Miss O'Reilly was locking her in her room?'

'What?' His faintly indulgent smile disappeared.

'As a form of discipline,' Miranda explained. 'I spoke to Justine about it, but she didn't seem at all concerned.'

The planes of his face hardened, until it looked like a carved mask. 'What in God's name am I supposed to do? Override both parents?'

'You'll have to!' Miranda shook her head from side to side. 'I don't like to see Andrea locked in for whatever reason, and you know as well as I do that whatever you say goes. Speak to Justine.'

'About what?'

Both of them, intensely preoccupied, had failed to notice Justine's almost feline approach.

'About Miss O'Reilly locking Andrea in,' Miranda said quickly, and now the colour raced under her translucent skin.

Justine stalked towards her, her black eyebrows raised. 'What on earth are you talking about?'

'We discussed it, Justine,' Miranda said quietly.

'The only thing we've discussed is your upsetting the best nanny we've ever had!' Justine corrected her sharply. 'For the short time you're here, Miranda, I must ask you not to do that. The burden of Andrea has been unbearable without Miss O'Reilly. Her methods might be strict, but there's no easy way with Andrea.'

'So she *is* locking her in?' Blake asked abruptly, with unmistakable distaste.

'As to that, I have no idea!' Justine turned her taut, thin body around to face Blake. 'I don't question Miss O'Reilly, Blake. She's made such wonderful progress with the child.'

'You mean she seems suddenly passive?' Blake's lancing blue gaze struck Justine's obviously unhappy face.

'I'm convinced Miss O'Reilly is helping her!' Justine argued. 'She's an expert in her field. She's a nurse and she knows the answers to difficult children's problems.'

'Bunkum!' Miranda said, unable to be silent any longer. 'What happiness is she bringing into Andy's life? You can't sort children out locking them up.'

'*Is* she?' Justine replied. 'I think you're just making that up.'

Blake brought his hand down firmly on Miranda's shoulder. 'You have no objection, Justine, if I speak to the woman tonight?'

'Why, of course not, Blake.' Justine fixed her long, narrow eyes pleadingly on his dark, unyielding face. 'I know she would like to speak to you.'

Blake glanced at the silent Miranda. 'Feeling better?'

'Yes,' she said huskily.

'God, you're accident-prone, aren't you?' Justine looked at her with open irritation. 'And *you're* the one who offered to look after Andrea!'

'If I were you, Justine,' Blake said rather shortly, 'I'd accept with gratitude.'

'I'm so on edge lately,' Justine ventured when she saw his dark expression. 'Mirry means well, but really she's such a child.'

'I really haven't got time to discuss it now.' Blake put two hands on Miranda's narrow waist and lifted her to the floor. 'Keep off that foot for the rest of the day.'

'The way you all fuss about her!' Justine's voice sounded strained. 'She looks so small and helpless, yet she's madly reckless.'

'She's pretty cool too in an emergency,' Blake said smoothly. 'Plenty of women would have hysterics if they were attacked by a savage animal. We've been hunting that dingo for months. I'm just sorry Miranda had to encounter it when it was wounded and doubly dangerous.'

'Well, she *would* ride out.' Justine seemed unable to hide her jealous hostility. 'I distinctly remember your telling her not to follow you too.'

After Blake had gone, obviously glad to be riding away, Justine turned to Miranda with a kind of burning anger. 'Don't you dare try to put me in the wrong with Blake!'

'Whatever do you mean, my dear?' Gran asked in a very polite voice.

'*She* knows,' Justine shook her sleek dark head. 'I really care what Blake thinks about me.'

'Well, yes,' said Gran, and turned her splendid head to look out over the garden. 'Miranda is a little impetuous, Justine, but it's clear to me she wants to help you.'

'I really can't see how!' Justine just stopped herself from snapping. That was how on edge she was.
No one, but no one raised their voice to Grandmother Seymour. She was a very privileged, very
damned superior lady, Justine thought, all the more
angry because the old lady had never let her in. *In*,
like pale blonde, pearly-skinned little Miss Miranda with her big green eyes.

'Why don't you let her keep Andrea company?'
Gran suggested. 'Did you know Andrea calls her
Sunshine?'

Justine shook her head, looking excessively
bored. 'The colour of her hair, I suppose.'

'She likes Miranda,' Gran said.

'What a compliment!' Justine stood up abruptly,
pencil-slim in her softest silk shirt and her skin-
tight yellow jeans. 'If it's going to make you happy,
Gran, Miranda can give Miss O'Reilly a helping
hand.'

'May I see her now?' Miranda asked.

'If it's absolutely necessary.' Justine's light
brown eyes flickered. 'You seem determined to
achieve something, Mirry, but Andrea will defeat
you. As for me, I'm going to paint.'

'She's clever too,' Gran commented, a few
moments after Justine had disappeared through the
door. 'Largely untaught, but she has real ability.'

'Yes, I know,' Miranda, who had an instinctively
good eye for art, agreed. 'When did she first start
to turn away from her only child?'

'From the beginning.' Gran looked down at her
hands, then ran her finger lightly over her magnificent sapphire and diamond ring. It was so tight
now, it never came off. 'Justine's paintings are

good, but they're not so nice. There's something tormented in her struggling to get out. She was like that before Andrea arrived. Almost from the moment she came into this house.'

Miranda wondered if she dared say what was on her mind, then decided she didn't. Besides, they both knew. Gran was highly intuitive, which made Miranda wonder in turn if Gran divined her own complex feelings for Blake.

Again Miss O'Reilly came to the schoolroom door.

'Good afternoon,' Miranda said in the voice she had been taught at her very exclusive girls' school.

'Good afternoon,' Miss O'Reilly returned, a little shaken to see Miranda back so soon.

'I thought I might mind Andrea for you for a while.'

'She's taking a nap.'

'All right,' Miranda said, 'I'll wait.'

'Wait?' Miss O'Reilly frowned.

It seemed to Miranda that tact and diplomacy were hopeless. She and Miss O'Reilly shared a mutual antipathy, and there was little use trying to circumvent it. She gazed back at this stern, highly qualified career lady, then managed to walk past her to the centre of the schoolroom.

'I used to do my lessons here.' Miranda turned to survey the large room where she had spent so much time.

'I gather you're a highly educated young lady.'

'Not really. A B.A.' Very gently Miranda touched the display case that housed a collection of beautiful Victorian dolls. These had come down from the daughters of the family and she supposed they were now quite valuable. She had loved them as a child. She still did, especially Kate.

'Splendid, aren't they?' Miss O'Reilly said with her first trace of warmth. 'The child takes no interest in them whatever yet I'm sure you loved them as a child.'

'But then she's never been allowed to touch them.'

'But of course not!' Miss O'Reilly seemed surprised. 'There are some wonderful examples there, so much to admire in the beauty and workmanship. A child like Andrea would obviously not know how to care for them.'

'You shouldn't dismiss her so soon, Miss O'Reilly,' Miranda said sadly. 'Andrea is surrounded by an abundance of everything, but precious few things is she allowed to touch. Touch is important.'

'Maybe so.' Miss O'Reilly smiled thinly. 'But you wouldn't suggest, surely, that she be allowed to play with any one of those exceptionally beautiful dolls?'

'She could be sorry for them because they're locked up.'

Miss O'Reilly walked away without another word. She went to the adjoining door, the old nursery and called: 'Andrea!'

Miranda soon joined her. 'I thought you said she was asleep?'

For answer Miss O'Reilly threw open the door. Andrea was there on the huge fourposter bed and only a quick glance confirmed that she was lying immobile, but wide awake.

Always on her visits back to Morning Star Miranda became very upset at her first sight of the child. She did seem to be retarded in that the normal responses of a four-year-old were scarcely present.

'You see?' Miss O'Reilly said. 'She'll never answer, but of course she hears perfectly.'

'Please, I'd like to speak to her on my own.'

'As you wish,' Miss O'Reilly said tersely. 'But her mother won't thank you if you set off another tantrum. I have them under control.'

Andrea still lay there as limp as a broken doll. She neither turned her head nor gave any indication that she cared that there were now two adults in her room, one of them Miranda, who knew well what it was like to be a lone child herself. No one could have been more generous or indulgent with Seymour money than Marcy, and though she had showered Miranda with gifts and toys and clothes, she had been temperamentally unable to give of her time.

After Miss O'Reilly had withdrawn, rigid with disapproval, Miranda walked to the window and looked out. The view from almost every window and French door in the house was superb—limitless vistas and close into the homestead a carefully maintained parkland, yet Andrea, whimpering, had almost to be forced outside. She was terrified of horses and almost as terrified of the cattle. Her father had long since decided she wasn't a Seymour at all, but some throwback in Justine's family. Someone she hadn't told him about.

'Hello, Andrea,' Miranda said gently, still looking across the vast expanse of lawn.

No reply.

'I'm hoping we can spend some time together.'

'You go *away*!' The gruff little voice was fierce and low.

'It isn't as though I want to,' Miranda said, 'but some things we just have to do. My mother died, Andrea. I can't live here any more.'

'Go away!'

Miranda couldn't decide whether the little girl meant her to go or whether she was repeating the last part of her sentence. From the pain-filled tone of her voice, Miranda decided she really wanted her to stay. In a way it *was* awful the way she hurt Andrea when she left, all the bottled up misery that reduced the child to speechless anger. It was even possible Miranda was now bothering her, yet Miranda felt absolutely committed to reach out to the child.

'Listen, Andrea,' she said. 'I'd like to take you to see the wildflowers—that's if you would like to come. They're so pretty, and we can tramp around all by ourselves. Of course you'll have to help me. I've hurt my foot.'

Andrea sat up on the bed and stared at her. 'Does it hurt?'

Miranda nodded her head, dipping it a little so she could swallow down the lump in her throat. Andrea was speaking to her with a great effort almost like someone whose vocal chords had been damaged. 'Not enough to stop us going out. It's my left foot, so I can drive the jeep.' Of course Blake had told her to stay at home, but she was hoping the glory of the desert gardens would have its effect. 'Would you like to see them?' she asked.

'Yes.' Andrea slipped off the bed, small for her

age, but compact. She wasn't at all a pretty child;
'a funny-looking little kid' someone had once de-
scribed her, and though she had Justine's colouring, dark hair and dark eyes, she bore not the
slightest resemblance to either parent. It was rather
a desperate little moon-face and Miranda felt
momentarily sick with emotion. 'What about *her*?'
Andrea asked, shooting a darting glance at the
connecting door.

'Are you worried about Miss O'Reilly?' Miranda
asked.

Andrea was silent.

'Gran said we might go.' Miranda put out her
hand.

Andrea surprised her by moving quickly and
taking her outstretched hand. 'Oh, one thing,'
Miranda said, 'we need shoes!'

'That's right.' The little girl looked up at her.

'Where are they, in the wardrobe?'

'That's right!' Andrea repeated in a sing-song
voice.

'Then we'll find them.' They walked together to
the huge red cedar wardrobe, and it suddenly
struck Miranda that the room, though beautiful
and big and airy, was too overpowering for a small
child. All the furniture was solid mahogany, mid-
Victorian, and though a teenager might have
thought the eight-foot high fourposter bed highly
romantic, it could have slept half a dozen four-
year-olds. Andrea might be finding it very difficult
to feel in control of such a large space. Then too,
there was an absence of colour, the bright primary
colours which could lift a child's mood. It was
really a sophisticated room, strongly formal, and

now that she thought about it, too big and lonely for a small child.

'Manda?'

Andrea was prompting her with a tug on her hand. Miranda stood there pondering no longer but opened the huge wardrobe and peered inside. There was an abundance of everything; so much Andrea couldn't possibly find time to wear, even if she changed several times a day. Very few of the little dresses Miranda would have chosen for her. They simply weren't Andrea's style, being pure Shirley Temple.

'What about these yellow ones?' She pulled out a pair of sneakers.

'Yellow,' said Andrea, and immediately plonked down so Miranda could put them on for her.

'*You* put them on, Andy.' Miranda put the right shoe into the child's hand.

Andrea's expression was significant; she looked pleased.

While Miranda waited she hadn't the slightest trouble putting on the sneakers, then tying the laces in a neat knot.

'Good girl!' Miranda looked her approval. 'Now let's go!'

There was another confrontation in the next room when Miranda decided they might take one of the dolls for an outing. Andrea faltered and showed signs of fright, but Miranda went to the cabinet and opened it.

'Which one, do you suppose?'

'Really, Miss Seymour!' Nanny expressed her disgust.

Andrea surprised both of them. She walked up

to the cabinet and put her hand out to reverently touch Kate's satin skirt. 'This one.'

'That's right!' Miranda smiled down at her. 'My favourite too!'

'In my opinion,' Miss O'Reilly said from behind them, 'you're creating additional problems. Andrea has a distinctly destructive streak.'

'I do hope,' said Miranda, 'she doesn't know the meaning of the word.'

The expression on Andrea's now glowering round face made it very clear she did.

Retarded! Miranda thought. She was well up in her vocabulary.

'I *hate* you!' she said.

'I'm sure you do,' Miss O'Reilly smiled, 'but very soon we shall be friends.'

'No. No. No. *No*!' The last was close to a scream.

'You've done it now.' Miss O'Reilly looked triumphantly into Miranda's dismayed face.

'We're going now, Andrea.' Miranda clasped the child's hand firmly. 'Would you like to carry Kate?'

'How foolish!' Miss O'Reilly obviously felt Miranda was doing the wrong thing.

'Please.' As soon as Miranda released her hand, Andrea held up her two arms.

'I can see she wants to come with us,' Miranda said. 'It's so stuffy in the cabinet. We'll take them all out, one by one.'

Andrea clasped the lovely doll tightly to her breast, deliberately avoiding looking at the nurse.

As an outing, it was a great success. All three sat quietly among the prolifically blossoming wildflowers, Andrea in utter absorption while she made chains of paper daisies to adorn first Kate, then Miranda, and finally herself. To Miranda's eyes she was displaying considerable manual dexterity and there was a definite pattern to her colour schemes.

The only time there was trouble was when they had to go home. Because the desert sunsets were so spectacular Miranda had deliberately delayed, but now they had to get moving so they could be home before dark.

'No, won't go!' said Andrea, bursting into tears.

It was difficult, watching her, not to pull the child on to her knee, but Miranda decided to be quiet and very gradual with her attentions. Andrea needed love desperately, but Miranda was very conscious that she wasn't Andrea's mother nor could she make the child emotionally dependent upon her. As Andrea had said herself: *You go away*.

'Don't forget Kate has to go home,' she said. 'Tomorrow we'll give Victoria a turn.'

Apparently that mattered, for the incipient tantrum turned off. 'Sorry, Kate,' Andrea told the doll.

'I'm sure she's enjoyed herself.' Miranda nearly felt like crying at the loving care Andrea was giving the doll.

'Because I love her,' Andrea explained.

All the way home she was very quiet, clutching the doll to her, but her expression was important. It was calm and almost hopeful, as if she foresaw other outings so pleasant and secure.

Justine was waiting for them, her exotic face not a whit pleased or relaxed.

'Andrea is late for her tea,' she said curtly.

Go jump in the drink! Miranda thought.

Andrea made an instant movement to clutch Miranda's hand, and as she did so, the doll slipped out of the crook of her other arm.

'Oh dear, you stupid girl!' Justine rushed suddenly to pick the doll up, staring at the bisque head for a crack.

Immediately Andrea began to cry; great heart-broken wails that brought Gran, then Blake out on to the porch.

'Who gave her the doll?' Justine shouted over the din.

'Miss Seymour did.' Nurse O'Reilly had materialised from nowhere.

'What for?' Justine screeched. 'She could have wrecked it!'

'*Please*, Justine,' Gran implored.

'I'll take Andrea upstairs,' said Miranda. 'She's taken the greatest care of the doll all afternoon. What happened then was an accident.'

'A behavioural problem.' Nurse O'Reilly instantly gave it another name.

'Damn it all, she breaks things!' Justine snapped.

'Here, baby!' Blake lifted the wailing child and set her up on his shoulder.

'*Oh!*' said Andrea, and stopped crying.

'Take her up, Blake,' said Gran. 'Miranda, you go too.'

'What's she trying to do?' Justine beseeched the old lady, obviously referring to Miranda. 'I've employed Miss O'Reilly here to look after the child, now Mirry seems dead set on aggravating the situation. What experience has *she* had in handling children? Andrea might like her, but that's not going to help much.'

Miranda continued to walk up the stairway in the wake of man and child. Andrea had two hands around Blake's neck, not holding on for dear life, but sitting easily.

As they reached the gallery she even turned her head and gave Miranda a fleeting smile.

Oh God, Miranda thought. What hope has this child got? It seemed to her in her suddenly downcast mood that Justine was largely responsible for all her little daughter's troubles. And how could anyone change that?

Blake planted the little girl on her bed and asked: 'Did you enjoy yourself today?'

'Will you let me take Victoria tomorrow?'

'Who's Victoria?' Blake asked.

'Victoria's another doll,' Miranda just stopped herself from sighing.

'Oh, I see!'

'May I, *please*, Blake?'

'Yes. But listen, you know you've got to look after her?'

The desperate little face visibly relaxed. 'I *know* I have to.'

'Then that's settled.' He stood beside the child, looking down at her quietly. 'Do you want your mother now?'

'No.' The expression was changing to anxiety.

'Are you happy with Miss O'Reilly, Andrea?'

'I hate her,' Andrea said.

Blake turned and looked at Miranda. 'Well, what do we do next?'

Andrea sat up, looking at them both with interest. The bed was so big and the child was so small, Miranda spoke her thoughts, her eyes sparkling with a zealous light. 'First, if you look around you, you'll see this room is too H-U-G-E!' She spelt out the last word.

'Don't like it,' Andrea said. 'Too *B-I-G*'

'How do you spell huge?' Blake asked.

Andrea looked at the fingers of her right hand. 'H-U-G-E,' she said.

'That's right,' Blake nodded. 'Would you like another room?'

'One you can pick yourself?' Miranda came to stand at Blake's shoulder.

'Oh, *yes!*' With a little animation, Andrea's stolid little face took on more character. 'One near Manda's.'

Blake nodded again. 'All right. You can pick your furniture as well.'

Andrea stared at him, big-eyed. 'No locks.'

'No locks, Andrea.'

Andrea's dark eyes filled with tears. 'No keys.'

'Whatever you want.' Blake put out his hand and smoothed her short hair. 'This is your house, Andrea.'

'*Your* house,' Andrea corrected, astonishingly like an adult.

'Then I'll give you anything you want, little cousin.'

Difficult, emotionally disturbed little Andrea launched herself at him crying incoherently, and Blake sat down on the bed and drew the child fully into his arms.

'Cry all over me, baby,' he said gently. 'Cry. Let it out.'

'That's the way you were with me,' Miranda said slowly, answering tears glittering in her green eyes. 'I love you, Blake,' she exclaimed. She sat down on the bed and while Andrea cuddled in his arms she laid her shining blonde head against his shoulder, nuzzling him like another child.

It was a strangely tender scene, and so good it had to be shattered.

'What the devil!' Justine's voice exclaimed from behind them.

Jarred back to reality, Miranda lifted her head, looking back at the furiously angry Justine. There she stood, a too-slim figure in her tight jeans and silk shirt, her dark eyes filled with anger and suspicion.

'Quietly now, Justine,' Blake instantly established his dominance, his voice soft yet very authoritative.

'How is she now?' Gran had entered the room, as ever aware of the crosscurrents.

'Fine.' Blake continued to hold the child, though her tears had stopped. 'We've discovered she doesn't like her room and she doesn't like Miss O'Reilly.'

'The only person who's had any success in handling her,' Justine said angrily.

'Miss O'Reilly hasn't helped her at all.'

The note of rebuke in Blake's voice made Justine whirl and fly out of the room.

'Oh dear, oh dear!' Gran looked after her in distress.

'Let her go, Gran,' Blake told her. 'Right now,

I'm more concerned with Andrea. So far as I'm concerned she has demonstrated tonight that there's not a damn thing wrong with her that plenty of understanding and affection can't cure.'

'I know that,' Gran looked directly at him, 'but most of it has to come from her *P-A-R-E-N-T-S*!'

'Then you ought to know, too,' there was a faint smile on Blake's firmly chiselled mouth, 'that Andrea can spell.'

'Yes.' Andrea drew away from Blake and nodded her head. 'And nobody taught me *anything*!'

After dinner Miranda waited quietly while Blake spoke to Miss O'Reilly in the library. It had been a very tense meal hour with no one saying very much at all. Justine had not eaten anything and Uncle Grant had kept his eyes fixed almost exclusively on his plate or the portraits of his ancestors. It was clear there had been an argument of sorts in their bedroom before dinner, and Miranda wondered yet again why Uncle Grant had ever imagined his marriage was going to work. They were like oil and water, the only point of similarity between them being that both of them were deeply disappointed in their only child. Miranda felt strongly that this was at the root of all Andrea's problems. How could any child accept not being loved and wanted? So she wasn't pretty? She had a long way to go. A lot of ugly ducklings turned into swans. But she was highly intelligent and hiding it, the tantrums and disturbed behaviour were desperate appeals for attention.

In the end, Miranda didn't eat much either, and now she waited outside the library door feeling rather sick and trembly. Blake had requested that she be there, and no one on Morning Star disobeyed Blake's requests.

A few moments later Blake opened the door, standing back so Miss O'Reilly could leave. That lady swept out, head high, dull uneven colour in her cheeks and a look in her eyes as they rested on Miranda of remarkable enmity.

Neither spoke. What was there to say?

'She's got it in for me!' Miranda observed wryly as soon as the library door was shut. 'Did you sack her?'

'She should never have been hired,' Blake said flatly. 'She might be able to sort some kids out, which I doubt, but not Andrea.'

'When does she leave?' Miranda wandered over to inspect the huge eighteenth-century English landscape atop the mantelpiece. It was a vision of quiet beauty, a sight well known to the early Seymours and as far removed from the strange, bizarre beauty of Morning Star as the craters of the moon.

'I'll have her flown out in the morning,' Blake said rather testily. 'I dislike having to do what should be taken care of by somebody else.'

'Uncle Grant won't speak,' Miranda said sadly. 'I think they had a fight.'

'A lot of married people have fights.' Blake stretched his long arms rather wearily. 'Personally I'm not hung up on the state of marriage at all.'

'That figures.' Miranda gave a little gurgle in her throat. 'But what about the heir to Morning Star?' Her emerald glance met Blake's with a kind of sweet malice.

'There has to be more to marriage than providing heirs.'

'What *is* it you set great store by?'

'I'm no longer sure,' his mouth twisted in what seemed to be self-mockery. 'You can't beat sensual pleasure.'

'Blake!' Miranda's delicate eyebrows rose. 'You mean you've found Val wanting?'

'Val would die for me.'

'Conceited beast!' As well he might be.

'Come over here,' he said, losing interest.

'Certainly.' She responded quickly to his businesslike expression, sitting down in the big winged-back chair opposite him so the light fell all over her hair and her face and the lightly ruffled, copper-pink dress she had on.

'You look outrageously pretty,' Blake said in a somewhat dampening tone.

'You know Gran likes us to dress for dinner.' Miranda looked down at herself, apologising hastily.

'Dressed, undressed, what's the difference?'

'Don't start *that* again!' she sighed heavily.

He gave a brief laugh that was edged with a faint violence. 'Your next fiancé, flower face, *I* pick.'

'And there's always the hope you'll pick a good one.' The excitement was rising in her, showing in the density of colour in her eyes, the colour that whipped up under her creamy skin. Any man would fall lamentably short of Blake.

'Haven't I always looked after you?' His look defied her to deny it.

'Of course you have.' She looked down and twisted her hands in her lap. 'I'm just sorry I can't pay you back. I mean, I had no idea about Marcy. . . . I would *never* have bought the Porsche. . . .'

'There *is* a way you can repay me,' Blake cut her off blandly.

'What?' She looked up, then flushed under his mocking gaze.

'Andrea's wellbeing means a lot to you, doesn't it?'

'Of course it does.' She actually got up and stood gazing down at him.

'You feel you understand her?' He tilted his head back against the chair, his blue eyes watching her.

'A little. You know—I have a certain way with children.'

'And men. Which is what we can do without.'

Tremors were starting to dance over her skin. He looked so indolent, yet she had the feeling it was masking a curious tension.

'What is it you want me to do?' She was driven to moving nearer.

'Stay here with Andrea.'

'For how long?' She couldn't break away from his lancing, pay-up-now look.

'For as long as it takes. Six months. A year. Until we can see quite clearly that she's calm and responsive. You've worked a small miracle already.'

'You did that, Blake,' Miranda told him.

'You seem worried.'

'Why not?' She gave him a speaking glance. 'You know as well as I do that I can't do this.'

'Why? No excitement. No thrills. No partying until three o'clock in the morning?'

'I want to help Andrea,' she cried. 'But you're forcing me.'

'I just thought you might want to show your gratitude,' he said dryly. 'What's a few months out of a butterfly's life?'

'All right, so I admit I've done nothing worth
while!' She turned on him in quick distress. 'But
Andrea's not my child. I can't just take her over.
Justine will have something to say.'

'Leave Justine to me.'

'Hell!' What a notion.

'What's that supposed to mean?' He reached out
suddenly and pinned her wrist.

'God knows!' Miranda looked down at him,
strangely transfixed. Blake had always had this
magnetism for her. Now she knew what it was.

'I hope you're not going to make something out
of nothing,' he warned her.

'What did I say?' He was hurting her.

'It's what you didn't say, kiddo.'

'So why are you getting angry?' she accused him.
'Could it be you're worried about something yourself?'

He stood up abruptly, towering over her. 'Don't
say any more,' he ordered, with icy disfavour. 'And
don't try to evade the issue. Do you want to help
Andrea or not? It's you or another nanny.'

She stared up at him, a little shaken. 'I've got to
get on with my life, Blake. I need work.'

'I'm offering you a job.'

'Are you?' she said wrathfully. 'I think you want
to keep me here on Morning Star.'

'That too.' He didn't even bother to deny it. 'Out
of my sight you seem to get yourself in a mess of
trouble.'

'It was Shane who got carried away, not
me.'

'What about the next guy?' he said with cool

contempt. 'I mean, *I* know I can kiss you breathless with passion.'

'And don't you love it!' she retorted, furious and humiliated because it was true.

'So if you need a little excitement I'm willing to supply it. Anything to keep you on the right track.'

'For God's sake!' Her tone implied that she knew he was making fun of her.

'An admirable situation, Miranda. You teach Andrea and I'll teach you.'

'No, thanks!' She went to turn away, but he caught her around the waist.

'What do you mean—no, thanks, you little hypocrite!'

'I've had enough lessons from you!'

'Life is all lessons.' Blake drew her back against him and put his arms around her like a cage.

She had difficulty just breathing. His body was warm; so too was the male scent of him. It was almost an act of ravishment just to be in his arms.

'If you want to prove anything,' she said bitterly, 'go ahead.'

'My own little Miranda!'

At the mockery in his voice the tears sprang to her eyes. Blake lowered his dark head until he found the pearly lobe of her ear.

'I want to eat you. Okay?'

She tried to shake her head, but it fell back against his shoulder. Her body was responding despite any directives from her brain. There was a humming sound in her head and her eyes closed while pleasure and pain got all mixed up inside her. She was being taken over by Blake in every way.

His mouth was slipping down the side of her neck and, barely able to stand, she turned her head so he could claim her mouth. There was no way she could control the raging flame within her; no way she wanted to try. Her actions were blindly instinctive; her body melting from the sizzling heat.

Somehow he had turned her and with his mouth still on hers, simply picked her up and walked back with her to the long, deeply cushioned sofa.

'Don't do this to me, Blake,' she whispered against his mouth.

'You know you want me to.'

"I don't know *anything*!' she tried to cry, but he simply didn't hear her, preoccupied with making his mastery of her consuming and total.

It wasn't difficult. Miranda had truly lost all sense of self. She was simply what Blake wanted of her. His mouth, his hands moved over her with stunning assurance. The blood was pounding in her ears, so tumultuously she thought she wouldn't stay conscious much longer. Though his hands smoothed her breasts, raising hungers she had never dreamed of, he made no attempt to bare them to his mouth or his tongue. He just touched them, and the excitement was so violent it was carrying her past sanity.

'Stop!' she gasped with her last breath. 'Don't torture me!'

He released her, looking down into her eyes. 'If you stop to think about it, I'm only kissing you.'

'It's too much!' The hunger inside of her was so insistent, so throbbing, it was pain.

He was still holding her down, his blue eyes

watching her very closely. Watching, *watching*. What was it he thought to see?

'Please, Blake. Someone could come in at any moment.'

'They'd have to knock first.' His tone was light, but it was apparent his emotions weren't under their usual impeccable control. The light eyes blazed and a pulse hammered in his temple. 'Are you sure you want me to stop?'

'I think you've punished me enough. You've had women falling for you for years, but you remain indifferent.'

'My come-uppance is bound to come!' His smile offered no apology. 'In any case, console yourself with the thought. I did show you you're not frigid. I never really believed you were.'

'Let me up!' His insolence put the strength back in her knees.

'I will as soon as you tell me you're going to stay.'

'Justine will be against it.'

'I daresay.' One finger traced her profile, making her lips quiver. 'But I can handle Justine.'

Isn't that just what she wants? Miranda thought, but let it pass.

'That's an alluring perfume you're wearing. What is it?'

'Me.' She hadn't had the time or inclination to dab herself with her favourite scent.

Blake laughed in his throat. 'God help the man who marries you! You'll sap his strength.'

CHAPTER SIX

FOR a week and more, Justine's mood was ugly, and Miranda bore the brunt of it in silence. Not that anyone was there to witness Justine's savagely jealous attacks on her; Justine wasn't that far gone that she would risk family condemnation. The bitter criticisms went on in private; sometimes when Andrea was there and when Miranda succeeded in diverting the child, sometimes not.

Now they were alone in Andrea's new bedroom, actually the old sitting room off Miranda's, and Justine was again venting her displeasure.

'Fancy allowing her to paint!' she said scathingly.

'You'd be surprised. She's very neat.'

'God, what a colour scheme!' Justine covered her eyes as though the sight of the bright yellow walls made her ill.

'She chose it herself.' Miranda put the paint-brush down. Her arm was aching and the smell of the gloss paint was rather overpowering.

'And you let her. It was nothing to do with me— nothing. I'm just the mother.'

'You're welcome to have a go.' Miranda indicated the primed wall from which she had stripped a very nice wallpaper not to Andrea's liking.

'Funny!' Justine seemed desperate to shout and scream at someone, and for the first time Miranda saw the resemblance between mother and child.

'Please believe I'm only trying to help,' she said gently, trying to deflect Justine's anger.

'Oh, you're helping all right. Helping *yourself*. Making yourself indispensable. Who knows, you could even be contemplating making a play for Blake!'

'I wouldn't have a chance.' Miranda said lightly.

'No, you wouldn't,' Justine gloated. 'A dizzy little blonde couldn't make Blake happy.'

'And *you* could?'

Justine flinched as from a blow. 'You bitch!'

'Don't take me for a fool. Tons of women fall for Blake. I'm not blaming you for it. In fact I understand and I'm sorry. But you made your choice, and if you worked at it, it could be a good one. Uncle Grant is a fine man.'

'I despise him,' Justine said.

'You married him for his money,' said Miranda, pitying her.

'I thought it would get me what I wanted. My parents were poor old battlers.'

'They're still alive?'

Justine nodded, her dark eyes staring at a point beyond Miranda's fair head. 'I couldn't bring myself to let the family meet them, so I told Grant they were dead.'

'*Oh!*' Miranda protested.

'Is it such a dreadful thing?' Justine flung at her. 'If you could see my mum you wouldn't expect her to have tea with Gran.'

'Why ever not?' Miranda's green eyes were searching.

'Don't be silly.' Justine slumped forward. 'Gran could take the mickey out of anyone.'

'Only as required.'

'My mum's just a stocky old bag.' Justine's thin, beautiful face wore an expression of outrage. 'I used to hate her when I was a kid. She was such a frumpy, and all the other mothers were so nicely dressed and well spoken. What looks I've got, I got from my dad. God knows what he ever saw in my mother.'

'Obviously something, if they're still together.'

'Who knows what keeps people together?' Justine pondered the cushion at her feet. 'That's why Andrea so sorely tries my patience. She's so like Mum.'

'She's like you too,' Miranda remarked a little tartly. Only she displays more sensitivity, more courage.

'Impossible.' Justine stood up. 'By the way, have you heard the news? Dear old Val is flying in with that botanist chap.'

'Stuart Radcliffe?'

Justine nodded. 'She's so much at ease with men—riding, shooting, flying, galloping through the bush. She must be getting pretty desperate by now. For all she throws herself at Blake, she can never get him to pop the question.'

'Maybe she'll do it this trip.'

'If I were free she wouldn't!' Justine said with something like a sob, and hurled herself from the room.

But of course she wasn't.

The following afternoon Valerie piloted in the well-known botanist in her father's light aircraft. She was an experienced pilot and by all accounts nerveless in an emergency. Only Blake, it seemed, reduced her to jelly. As she watched them together, Miranda's tender heart smote her. Valerie's feelings were transparently, pathetically clear: her face flushed, her full mouth faintly trembling, her eyes brilliant with some inner vision; herself at Blake's side. Miranda thought how surprised she would be if it all came off. Blake didn't need women. Not like that. He was totally self-sufficient, and Valerie would end up with a broken heart. Whoever followed Gran as mistress of Morning Star would be someone far different from Val.

'What are you looking so profound about?' Stuart Radcliffe asked quietly in her ear. He was a tall, loosely knit man in his late forties, distinguished in his field, and perhaps because of it acutely observant. Now his pale blue gaze was ranging over Blake, so vivid and dominating to the thoroughly enraptured Valerie at his side. She was telling him something eagerly and he gave her shoulder an encouraging little pat. Miranda herself had had plenty of those pats, but she had never accepted them as visible signs of devotion. They were simply take-it-or-leave-it signs of approval, or keep-up-the-good-work or whatever.

'Will they or won't they make a match of it?' Stuart enquired.

'Your guess is as good as mine,' Miranda answered in the same low, measured tones. 'How was the trip?'

'Splendid!' Stuart said firmly. 'What a truly efficient woman she is. Together with her looks and eminent suitability it should put her well in the running—yet I have a gut feeling that Blake is immune to her charm.'

Miranda walked mechanically on. Valerie, as yet, had not deigned to acknowledge her, but she wasn't all that worried. Valerie was playing a part now; that of Blake's long-intended bride-to-be, a vision people were not really supposed to see through.

For dinner Valerie looked handsome and Justine looked dangerous and Stuart seemed vastly interested in everyone. This was his fourth or fifth visit to the station and what a fantastic place it was! Outside in the brilliantly star-crowded night the sound of tapsticks and native drums carried across the timeless land; primitive, all-pervasive, thrilling, enough to send the tourists goggle-eyed, yet inside the great fortress-like homestead it was clear that civilisation prevailed. Old Mrs Seymour was very splendidly got up and the younger women, with the exception of young Miranda, were effectively dressed to kill. Watching her, Stuart decided she was the nearest human thing to a flower, exquisite in her purity and innocence. For Blake he had a great respect and liking. Many cattle barons exuded power and authority, but not all of them were so sophisticated in its true sense, nor so generous with their money and time. The old lady asking him a question put an end to his observations.

It was Valerie who suggested they might have a look at the corroboree the station blacks were staging at Stallion Creek. Aborigines were superb natural dancers and all of them had seen dramatic exhibitions that stirred up the oddest sensations in body and mind. One of the young station hands, Billy, was a noted dancer and held in great respect

for his artistry, and as Blake looked down into
Valerie's brilliant laughing face he remarked that
for her sake he hoped Billy wasn't too tired, after a
long day's mustering, to take part in the performance.

The word spread like wildfire that the Byamee
and his guests were to be in the audience, and as
they arrived at the creek in the station wagon a
long welcoming chant rang out.

'Oh, I say!' Stuart looked around at the bizarre
beauty of the scene.

'It quickens your pulse, doesn't it?' Miranda
smiled at him.

'It does indeed.'

An elder of the tribe had advanced on Blake,
seething with dignity and pride, welcoming him and
his people to the Dance of the Blue Crane.

'Fascinating chap, isn't he?' Stuart inclined his
head to the petite Miranda.

'Old Wally?' She named the tribal elder.

'Actually I meant Blake. He's no ordinary man.'

'No.' In the light from the main fire Blake looked
well qualified to be a kind of god to these people.
So few people had presence, the magnetic quality
that set them apart and above the group. Blake
had it in full measure; not just his striking good
looks—Uncle Grant, for example, was still a handsome man—but his aura, the strength and the
grace, the easy assumption of power. Was it so
extraordinary that Justine, exposed to such un-
imagined dangers, should fall madly in love with
him? It was all part of some terrible pattern. Uncle
Grant had never brought Justine back to Morning
Star until after their whirlwind marriage. Justine

could not seriously have anticipated someone like
Blake. Above the orange-gold flame of the fire
Miranda quietly studied the two women who
flanked Blake's tall figure like handmaidens: Valerie, in a fluid column of white jersey, happy and
excited; Justine, wretched, like the wicked en-
chantress in red.

Stuart patted her arm and she jumped. 'I hope I
didn't crush you in the car?'

'Not at all.' Her eyes in the light of the fire were
glittering like jewels. 'I think we're in for a treat
tonight. That's Billy, their main dancer, all dressed
up like a fantasy. He's the brolga, the blue crane.'

Half laughing at something Valerie had said,
Blake spread out one of the two rugs he had
brought with him to protect the women's light
dresses. That done, he moved over to where Miranda and Stuart were hovering.

'Take this, flower face,' he ordered Miranda
to take one end of the plaid-patterned woollen
rug.

'Here?'

'A bit further over.' He gave her a sharp glance.

Surely he didn't think she was planning a little
interlude with Stuart? she thought defiantly. Stuart
might have been a bachelor and a very pleasant,
personable man, but as far as Miranda was concerned he belonged to another generation.

Finally they were all seated and the performance
began.

'Doesn't the woodsmoke smell delicious?' Miranda whispered to Stuart.

Valerie turned her dark head to give Miranda a
deliberate, quelling glance and Stuart touched

Miranda's arm and smiled. 'No talking in the stalls!'

Songmen and women were grouped near the didgeridoo artists and the tapsticks and the sand drums were already building up to a powerful cacophony of sound. Now the women began to chant and with dramatic suddenness the Blue Crane swept out from the trees and touched down in the central arena.

'Good grief, isn't *he* good!' Stuart, like Miranda, was a compulsive talker, but as a guest was spared Valerie's disapproving glances.

'I've seen him dance some wonderful roles.' Miranda moved closer so she and Stuart could carry on a confidential chat.

'Superb!' Stuart breathed.

With his feathery wings outstretched and his brown slender feet scarcely touching the ground Billy gave the appearance of floating around the circle of fires. Then he stopped, poised on one leg looking down into the imaginary Blue Lily lagoon. So realistic was his pose, one could see the bird.

'Who works out the choreography?' Stuart lowered his head to whisper in Miranda's ear.

'This is a very old dance. Very, very old. Billy has been tutored in the steps since his initiation.'

'Miranda, *please*!' Valerie looked back to give Miranda a baleful look.

'Naughty, naughty!' Stuart remarked kindly through his teeth.

'Come over here, Miranda, so I can keep an eye on you,' said Blake.

From her startled expression, Valerie didn't like that one bit, and Miranda discovered in herself the sudden urge to annoy her further. Who did she think she was, anyway? What arrogance! That was the worst of some heiresses—the way they were determined to keep other people in order.

'I'm going to be even naughtier,' Miranda told Stuart in a hurried aside, then rose gracefully to her feet. If Valerie was going to treat her like a little girl she would act like a little girl and curl up in Blake's lap.

It was the kind of thing calculated to send both Valerie and the remote-looking Justine quite mad. While the story of the Blue Crane unfolded and the rows of songmen took up a soaring chant Miranda leaned first sideways against Blake, then when her curls were tickling his chin, he put an arm around her and drew her right back against his shoulder.

'Perfect!' she breathed, and totally relaxed.

Justine looked as if she could attack her with her nails and Valerie took no further notice of the dance. It was a pity in a way, because everyone connected with the performance seemed to be on some kind of high. Billy's elevation, for instance, would have turned Nureyev green.

The smell of the woodsmoke was almost narcotic, tanging the nostrils; so too was the rich and rhythmic droning voices of the didgeridoos. It wasn't soothing music at all, but music to make the nerves jump. A breeze sprang up and the fires flickered, and right at that moment the women broke into the beautiful, shivery, wind-in-the-leaves chant.

'*Oh!*' Miranda felt the shiver pass through her own body and Blake looked down at her and tightened his arm. Now it wasn't so easy to play her part. Proximity to Blake was taking its toll. If they were only there together! But it was useless to think about it.

It was almost midnight, but these children of the Dreamtime were prepared to go on for hours, continuing without rest until dawn.

'I think we should go,' Valerie suddenly announced. 'I only intended to stay an hour.'

Curled against Blake and looking very young and fragile, Miranda urged her to wait until the Blue Crane had flown away.

'I think not!' Valerie was thoroughly rattled by the rhythmic chanting.

'It's almost over,' said Blake, expressing his wish that they should stay. 'I've seen this ballet since I was a boy, but I've never seen it performed better.'

'Splendid!' Stuart seconded, hypnotised by the whole thing. 'That Billy fella would light up any stage!'

A few minutes later, while the chanting swelled to a triumphant climax, the joyful bird turned in the direction of the white man's presence, outstretched its wings with tremendous fluid grace, then leaping in the air soared away in the direction of the trees.

The drums ceased, the tapsticks, the droning and the chants. The ballet came to a close while a complete hush fell over the whole assembly.

It was good theatre, and all the way back to the homestead Stuart marvelled at the utter professionalism. 'A thoroughly enjoyable performance.'

'May I come out with you tomorrow, Stuart?' Miranda asked.

'Why, of course you may. Your knowledge of the country alone will be immensely valuable.'

'I'd like to bring Andrea with me.'

To his credit Stuart didn't even hesitate. 'If you're sure she would like to come.'

Justine, seated in the middle, between Uncle Grant and Stuart, looked furiously angry. 'I think it would be a good idea if you left Andrea behind.'

'She loved being out among the wildflowers,' Miranda pointed out gently, from her cushioned perch in the luggage compartment. Anything was better than being squashed up against the simmering Justine. 'She could learn so much watching Stuart.'

'You mean get in his way.'

'Not really,' Stuart said soothingly. 'I'm particularly interested in all the little plants that are growing in the normally bare areas, such as the hill country. Blake tells me some have sprung up that he's never seen before.'

'Classifying plants can't be an easy task,' Uncle Grant remarked, obviously trying to get his wife off a difficult subject, and to help him out Stuart immediately launched into instances where the experts had been fooled.

Back at the homestead Valerie decided she needed supper. Naturally reed-slim, she was nevertheless the possessor of a very healthy appetite.

'Cook will have gone to bed,' Justine offered stiffly.

'That's perfectly all right!' Valerie's colour rose a little at Justine's tone, but she still managed to smile. 'I'm quite gifted in the kitchen, you know.'

'I *loathe* it!'

'Then it's just as well you've come to your dream house.'

This definitely rated as an insulting remark and Miranda felt embarrassed on Justine's account. Then she remembered Justine had told no one about her background. Looking at her, so obviously a hothouse flower, perhaps a beautiful, faintly sinister orchid, one would have thought she had always known riches and lived in a big, beautiful house. Valerie would have found that 'battler' background a revelation and found the odd minute to be hateful about it. Valerie really was a terrifying snob. So was her mother, but not so nice Angus.

While the others went off, Uncle Grant caught Miranda's arm. 'May I have a word with you, Mirry?'

'Of course, Uncle Grant.' She looked up at his handsome, distinguished face thinking it very strange that although he resembled Blake's late father very closely he completely lacked the dynamic quality, the ruthless strength if they needed it, that so characterised his brother and nephew.

'Come into the drawing room, then.'

'Yes?' When they were seated she lifted her young, innocent, lovely face.

'Do you think it wise to upset Justine, my dear?' he asked in a calm, kindly tone.

'That's the last thing I'm trying to do, Uncle Grant.'

'You don't see that you're doing it. I know you're the kindesthearted child in the world. But the fact is, you're upsetting her dreadfully.'

'Oh, *no*!' Miranda dropped her shining head

with its aureole of curls.

'Please, dear. I don't want to upset you. I'm very fond of you, as you know.'

'What is it I'm doing, Uncle Grant?' Miranda braced herself instinctively.

'I know you're intending no such thing, but Justine has the notion that you're trying to discredit her in Blake's eyes.'

'Good grief!' Miranda said soberly.

Uncle Grant too fell silent, then he spoke. 'We had a long talk before dinner.'

Argument, you mean, Miranda thought with resignation.

'I know Blake sent that woman away and quite frankly I'm glad, but Justine did hire her and she feels, not without reason, that she was getting results. I don't think you realise just how bad Andrea has been. Did you know she broke the Ming vase?'

'Yes, I did.'

'Mother never said a word, and that vase was a treasure irreplaceable!'

'No object, no possession is as important as a human being,' said Miranda firmly.

'What do you mean by that, dear?'

Miranda lifted her great green eyes and they were shining with tears. 'Uncle Grant, don't you know your little daughter has been desperately unhappy?'

'Darling, darling, do you think *I* haven't been unhappy?' Uncle Grant demanded, his face working. 'I would give anything to hear little Andrea say she loves me, but there doesn't seem to be any response, any sweetness, any gentleness in her. Why, who would forget you at the same age? Such a joyous, perfect child. It grieves me deeply that my little one was born a disturbed child.'

'She wasn't born that way,' Miranda said quietly, not wishing to hurt him, but fighting for Andrea. 'You've seen all the doctors. There's nothing wrong with her that the right kind of loving attention can't fix.'

'But we *all* love her!' Uncle Grant protested. 'I was thrilled out of my mind to become a father. You can't imagine. I thought I was always going to remain a bachelor. No woman moved me outside my dear little lost love except Justine.'

'Oh, Uncle Grant!' Miranda felt like crying hysterically. As a young man Uncle Grant had been engaged to a very beautiful English cousin who had been killed in a riding accident on the property less than a month after her arrival in Australia. The tragedy had caused them all acute suffering, but none more than the young Grant who had adored her and held her in his arms as she died.

'My little Sarah!' he said as though it were all yesterday.

Miranda took his hand and he bent sideways and kissed her cheek. 'Bless you, you're only a baby, yet you understand.'

'I know what it is to love, Uncle Grant, and I know what it is to be denied that love. Andrea will come right. She *will* be happy, and so will you. It's just going to take a little time and the desire of everyone around her to help.'

'But must we upset Justine?' Uncle Grant sighed. 'In her own way she's just as remote as Andrea.'

'They do share certain characteristics,' Miranda confirmed slowly.

'She feels it's too much of a responsibility to leave Andrea to you. After all, you're only a young girl with no experience of children.'

'The fact is,' Miranda said hardily, 'I'm succeeding with Andrea. She likes me, Uncle Grant. She trusts me. She knows I'm her friend. I'm not going to let her down. The way Miss O'Reilly got results was through intimidation.'

'Oh, come now, Miranda. . . .'

'We can't evade it. As a form of discipline she was locking Andrea in her room, and she hated it.'

'Did she expect to be let out to be more destructive?' Uncle Grant frowned now, well used to Andrea's tantrums in the past.

'Miss O'Reilly took her freedom away from her. You've seen wild horses. What do *they* do when they're captured? Some of them will kill themselves rather than be taken. What about those range-bred brumbies that went into the gorge? Freedom is the most important thing in the world—freedom to come and go. Andrea suffered torments being locked in her room.'

'It's not exactly a prison,' Uncle Grant pointed out self-protectively.

'It was to her. In any case, as soon as we've finished painting she's moving down to my old sitting room. It's just her size and she's taken a very intelligent interest in our plans to furnish it.'

'Justine doesn't approve,' Uncle Grant pointed out.

'You look like you do.'

'We can't take it upon ourselves to upset Justine and override her wishes.'

'Damn it all, Uncle Grant, you're the father!'

A flush rose to Uncle Grant's lean, darkly tanned cheeks. 'I think you're calling me a bad one.'

'No, no.' Miranda put her head on his shoulder. 'I can see it all—your disappointment with Andrea, your wish not to upset Justine, but for everyone's sake, you must act and act now. If you don't, we run the risk of crippling Andrea further.'

'Dearest little girl, could you be the best judge?'

'I *know*, Uncle Grant. I know what it's like to hurt inside. I'll never forgive Marcy—oh, forget it!'

Uncle Grant looked at her, appalled. 'I suppose all our love never made up for Marcy's deficiencies as a mother?'

'No.' It was a soft little tormented sound. All her life since her father had been killed Miranda had had to turn to someone else but Marcy for comfort and attention. The number of times she had thrown a strangling grasp around Gran's neck, Blake's. . . .

'What is it you want me to do?' he asked quietly.

'Be what you are, a master of diplomacy. Smooth over Justine's anxieties, but you'll have to side with me. Andrea wants a new bedroom. She wants outings and lots of indoor and outdoor activities. Things can be pretty overwhelming sometimes to a four-year-old, but so far she's reacting quite well. I just act casual, matter-of-fact, and before I know it, she's joined in. Maybe God's helping me, Uncle Grant, directing me. I do so want to do something worth while. My own life up to now has been a bit of a mess, with Blake always charging in to rescue me.'

'Listen, sweetheart, he enjoys it,' Uncle Grant gave her a quick hug. 'There's a very romantic side to Blake. He would have made a dream of a knight.'

At that, Miranda smiled. 'Are you going to help me, Uncle Grant?'

'If I don't, my name's not Seymour. We had a few knights of our own!'

CHAPTER SEVEN

BECAUSE of Andrea's great fear of horses exploration of the hill country was abandoned for the following day. There they would need the horses, whereas they could take the jeep out to the desert fringe.

'You're being awfully good about it, Stuart,' Miranda told him.

'Not a bit of it!' Stuart bestowed a beaming smile on the small child. 'I say, I like that hat.'

'I dec'rated it myself.'

And so she had, with white and gold bachelor's buttons.

'Well, come on, girls!' Stuart was anxious to be off. 'Haven't forgotten the picnic basket, have you?'

'Oh, no!' Andrea looked quite shocked. 'Cook's made me a million sandwiches and I can have a lolly if I eat them all up.'

This sounded perfectly normal, and Stuart bent and scooped the child up. 'Right—oh, Miss Seymour, you can show me which way to go.'

It was a beautiful day, with not a single thing going wrong. While Stuart made his notes and sketches and collected specimens for closer observation and drying Andrea bent over the thick white paper Miranda had brought along with her and unhesitatingly began to draw.

'Good idea, that,' Stuart commented absentmindedly. All kiddies loved making coloured scrawls. It had a calming effect on their minds.

Andrea didn't need any encouragement. Now that Miranda had started her she had discovered in herself a direct means of self-expression. She might never be a chatterer, but the coloured crayons swiftly covered the blank pages in such a way that Miranda decided she would wait until Stuart had finished his own work to show him what a supposedly slow and disturbed four-year-old had done. Painting just simply did not appeal to Andrea; the urge and capacity to do so was as strong as the need for salvation.

Now and again Andrea looked to Miranda to see her reaction, and although Miranda smiled, she made no comment. It wasn't particularly easy to assess Andrea's work except to say that for a four-year-old, it was brilliant. In among the flowers and the faithfully reproduced flat-topped mesas there were human figures—male, female and realistic enough to be fairly easily identified. Just looking at them made Miranda feel decidedly uncomfortable. There was a lot of anger in Andrea's little soul.

'With any luck at all,' Stuart was saying, 'I'll be able to fit in the art sites. It's such spectacular country, isn't it, in its savage way? The mineral strata along the gorges fascinate me; the way they change colour in the sun. They tell me Stallion Creek has been a meeting place for aborigines for untold centuries.'

'Like Mary,' said Andrea, indicating that she had been listening to the conversation. Mary was the little aboriginal housegirl who sometimes served Andrea her meals.

'Good Lord!' Stuart had only just seen Andrea's complex drawing.

'I knew you'd be interested.'

Stuart's face didn't only express interest, it expressed amazement. 'Here is a gifted child.'

'And nobody taught me,' Andrea remarked.

'I think we'll have lunch now,' Miranda announced. For the time being Andrea might as well accept her gift as ordinary.

'Beauty!'

Just a simple word, but accompanied by a big smile. Miranda considered Andrea had changed enormously.

'You'll have to help me set it up.'

Instantly Andrea put away her crayon, then jumped to her feet.

'What an interesting child!' said Stuart.

At home late that afternoon Gran turned the pages of Andrea's coloured drawings over one by one.

'Dear God!' she said in a prayerful tone.

'Isn't she wonderful, Gran?' Miranda looked steadily over the old lady's shoulder.

'You too.' Gran caught at Miranda's hand. 'Remember none of us knew anything about it.'

'I can't take the credit,' Miranda returned the pressure of the old lady's hand. 'Andrea has inherited her ability from her mother.'

'But you, my dear child, wrought the small miracle. Respect your own ability. You succeeded where nobody else has, and in a remarkably short time. You've been the only person Andrea has been able to relate to. Don't think *I* haven't desperately tried. Andrea is happier than she's ever been in her whole life.'

'Gran——' Justine appeared at the door of Gran's sitting room with an outraged expression on her face.

'Yes, dear?' Gran turned her regal head.

'Whoever put Mary in charge of Andrea?'

'*I* did,' said Miranda in surprise.

'But, my dear girl, I *can't* have Mary looking after Andrea!'

'Why ever not, dear?' Gran intervened.

'For one thing, I'm not going to abandon my child to an illiterate little half-caste.'

'Oh, no, Justine,' Gran said quietly. 'Mary was educated on the property. She's an intelligent, good girl and it saddens me to hear you speak of her so disparagingly.'

'I've been taught the blacks were no good.'

'By whom?' Gran said icily.

'By . . . *everyone*!' Justine made a frenzied little gesture in the air. 'I remember that maniac stockman.'

'Then you'll remember the brain tumour that killed him was brought on by a severe head injury. One of our horses did that. We depend upon our aboriginal stockmen. They work zealously to keep Morning Star what it is.'

'I'm sorry, Gran,' Justine's dark eyes were filled with tears—not of remorse, but frustrated rage. 'I simply don't want a little aboriginal girl looking after my only child.'

'In that case, my dear, might you not be responsible for her yourself?'

With glittering eyes Justine took herself off.

'What are we going to do?' Indomitably Gran rested her face in her hands.

'Won't Uncle Grant take Justine away for a holiday?' suggested Miranda.

'No.' Gran straightened, shaking her snow-white head. 'Nothing will take Grant away from Morning Star. Nothing. Not even the fact that his wife hates it.'

'No one could hate Morning Star. Find it lonely, perhaps.'

'Yet there might be no alternative,' Gran sighed. 'It consoles me to think I can talk to you, Miranda. You're family and I trust you.'

'Shall I go after Justine?' asked Miranda.

'It won't, hurt her to mind her own child,' Gran said dryly.

'I'll go all the same,' Miranda exclaimed. 'Just when we were thinking of showing the drawings to her too.'

'Take them now.' Gran held the pile of drawings up.

'I hate you—hate you—hate you!' Andrea was screaming through the open schoolroom door.

Miranda picked up her heels and flew down the corridor just in time to hear the sound of a hard slap.

'You ugly, *stupid* little girl!'

In the doorway Miranda stopped with a jolt. Mary was there, looking terrified, Andrea four-square brazen with a red stain on her cheek, Justine leaning over her, possibly thinking of striking the child again.

'Justine!' Miranda cried.

'So you're here, are you?' Justine fumed. 'What

a fool I was to give in to Blake's request! You're hopeless with Andrea.'

'In what way?' Miranda couldn't resist saying it.

'Shouting at me like a little wild animal!'

'You may go now, Mary,' Miranda told the distressed little coloured girl.

'Who's giving the orders around here?' Justine shouted. 'I'm senior to you. I'm Mrs Grant Seymour.'

'Thank you, Mary,' Miranda said quietly.

'Yes, miss.' Gratefully Mary withdrew from the room.

'You wish you had power, don't you?' Justine cried. 'Damn you, don't you give orders while I'm here!'

'Andrea, why don't you see if the paint's dry?' The tears on Andrea's round cheeks weren't the tears of a child.

'I've been bad, Manda.' Andrea suddenly choked. 'I'm mean and bad and ugly.'

'You can stop that any time you want. You're a person, a growing-up little person. You're ready to take responsibility for yourself. You can shout or you can do as I ask you. It's your decision.'

Andrea stared at her with pain-filled wide eyes. 'There are so many different things to do.'

'Yes. You can decide. You can be mean or you can do better things—paint, talk to people, learn about life and growing up.'

'I'll see if the paint's dry,' said Andrea. 'No one is going to be allowed into my room except you and me.'

'Satisfied, are you?'

Justine appeared to be foully, insanely jealous.

'Please let's be calm about this, Justine,' Miranda pleaded. 'There's something I want to show you.'

Justine shook her head. 'I could tolerate you when you were younger, Mirry, but nowadays I don't like you at all.'

'Why not, what have I done? I'm still the same person.'

'No, you're not!' Justine gave her a peculiar smile. 'Even dear Valerie's nose is pretty much out of joint. That was quite an act you put on with Blake last night.'

'I don't understand.'

'Oh yes, you do!' There was a cynical look in Justine's long, Egyptian eyes. 'Do you suppose one woman doesn't know all about the other? Especially women in love. And you love Blake, don't you? You did as a child. He was so brave and handsome and dashing—but now it's different. You've discovered sexuality, something about yourself you didn't know. You not only love Blake, you're madly in love with him.'

'Can't we get back to Andrea?' Miranda said.

'You don't deny it, do you?'

'You mean to believe it whatever I say,' Miranda pointed out ruefully. 'In any case, Justine, Val and Blake seem to get on extremely well.'

'Very likely. But what she's got doesn't matter most to a man. Not a man like Blake with strong passions. Do you really believe he wouldn't have carried her off if he loved her?'

'Maybe he wants to see if she can handle the job. It's no easy thing to run the homestead and keep all the staff happy. One has to have the right touch.'

'She just loved what you did to her last night. Cuddling up to Blake, taking all his attention. He regards you as a pretty child, a sort of little sister.'

'I just want you to look at Andrea's drawings,' said Miranda. 'Let me show you.'

But Justine was already on her way to the door. 'I'm quite sure you've touched them up.'

'Justine, I can't draw for nuts.' Miranda made a desperate attempt to win her. 'Please stop and look. She did them today. Stuart and I think they're quite remarkable.'

'For a poor little thing like Andrea, I suppose.' Very deliberately Justine turned her back on Miranda and, in doing so, on her daughter.

In the morning it was discovered that a valuable mare was gone and this set off a commotion.

'What's going on, what's wrong?' Gran asked when Blake came back to the house for his gun.

'Columbine's gone.'

'Taken, we think, by a brumby stallion!' Valerie followed him in, lithe and purposeful. 'Of course we'll have to go after her.'

'Can I come?' Miranda called down the stairs.

'You'd only be in the way,' Valerie glanced at Blake. 'Some of the boys have seen that stallion. It's so big for a brumby it stands out.'

'Please, Blake,' Miranda persisted.

To her surprise he nodded curtly. 'All right. We'll be riding all over, but you can stay with me.'

Only then did Miranda think of Andrea, and Gran saw it in her eyes. 'Don't worry about Andrea, dear. There are enough women in the house to look after her for a few hours.'

'It could take longer than that, Gran.' Blake came back from his study, his expression grim. 'If it's the stallion we're thinking about, he's a rogue. One of the colts we rounded up had been savaged and Kenny came on a dead wild stallion only six weeks ago. It had been battered to death.'

'Take care,' said Gran, as ever.

Twenty minutes later, six of them were riding in the direction that Abe, their black tracker, had selected. Abe was an expert in following any kind of tracks, human or animal, and of necessity their progress was fairly slow.

'I can't think why you came.' Valerie rode up beside Miranda. 'The sun is gaining in strength all the time.'

'I won't melt.'

Valerie gave her a look of displeasure. 'Personally I don't think you'll go the distance. You haven't ridden for some time. You won't be able to mew like a kitten when your bones begin to ache.'

'Don't worry about me, Valerie,' Miranda said a little sharply, 'I'm tougher than I look.'

'Really?' Valerie gave her a faintly pitying stare. 'Every time you come here you seem to do some damned imbecile thing.'

'Is there anyone you don't sell short outside yourself?' Miranda asked promptly. 'I may be the poor relation, but you must have noticed that Gran and Blake don't treat me like one. Keep up your digs and I swear I'll tell them.'

Valerie gave her a most peculiar look from under the wide brim of her hat. 'I'm sorry if I offended you. I didn't intend to.'

'You must make more effort to be pleasant.' Miranda smiled sweetly and rode up.

Mid-morning they came on two young studs running together.

'Half-brothers,' said Blake, his sapphire eyes slitted against the mirage. 'Sired by the same father out of two different mares, their markings are so much alike.'

'Isn't it extraordinary how like people they are?' As always Miranda was entranced by the sight of running wild horses. 'They form attachments just like we do. They're affectionate and loyal and jealous. The males dominate the females, and the male's protective instinct is very strong. Stallions even have predilections for mares of a certain colour, like some men prefer blondes. I think it's fantastic.'

Valerie cut off Miranda's musings rather shortly. 'Surely they're going too deeply into the stallion's territory?'

'We're not even sure if it *is* his territory,' said Blake. 'There could be several stallions in the area. We don't know which one took Columbine.'

'On the other hand,' Uncle Grant offered, 'Kenny and the boys found the dead stallion not far from Eight-Mile Creek. It must have been a pretty savage fight. Normally stallion fights don't go beyond the display stage.'

'That one did,' Blake said grimly. 'It must be the big mahogany stallion. Few of the wild stallions I've seen would be capable of defeating and killing another stallion in its prime. It was a fight to the death. That's what worries me. We're dealing with a particularly powerful and brutal rogue. Colum-

bine would try to get back to her own territory
and the stallion may damage her trying to herd her
back into the ranks. She's a very valuable mare.'

'Maybe those two colts will lead us to *our* stallion!' Chilla, Blake's foreman, had now joined
them, sitting his horse like the rest of them as they
stared away in the direction of the frisking colts.
'They look—what, three, four?'

'Probably.' Blake accepted this as an estimate of
the colts' maturity. 'They don't look anywhere near
strong or aggressive enough to challenge a fairly
dominant stallion.'

'Nevertheless it's been done before, boss.' Chilla
swept off his slouch hat and wiped the sweat from
his brow with the back of his hand. 'A couple of
young studs just could ambush a stallion.'

'If it's the stallion that took Columbine, they've
got no hope. They're still too young to defeat a
stallion and take over a harem. They'll be six or
seven before they do that. However, the stallion
might just come out and drive them off. In which
case, we'll be waiting.'

'You're not going to shoot him, are you, Blake?'
Miranda protested.

'I'll know when the time comes. It was easy
enough to take Columbine. He'll be back to take
more of the mares and fillies away, and I can't
allow that to happen. This is a question that has to
be settled.'

'Can't you just drive him away?'

'No.' Blake answered without hesitation. 'We'll
ride downwind of the colts and see what happens.'

'Why don't you turn back?' said Valerie to Miranda as the men headed off. 'This could be a lot

more strenuous than you think.'

'I didn't think it was going to be a garden party.' Miranda's green eyes had a cool look. 'Come on, let's catch up to the men.'

It was a long ride leading them into the lignum swamps where the colts had a beautiful little filly stashed away.

'This is it,' said Blake. 'The stallion will pick up the filly's scent and come after her. She's a chestnut too, no possible match for Columbine, but in the same colour range.'

'She looks as if her own sire has just driven her off.' From their position downwind Miranda was studying the little filly closely. 'Otherwise how did the colts pick her up?'

'She could be the stallion's own daughter,' Valerie said quickly.

'I don't think so.' Blake too was staring at the perfect little filly with its chestnut coat and deeper red-brown mane and tail. 'I think we'll find our killer is the dark mahogany with the black mane and tail.'

Just at that moment, a young part-aboriginal stockman, expending some of his super-abundant energy, galloped out of the lignum like a bolt from the blue.

'God *damn* it!' Blake cursed, but not before the two colts and the filly sprang into an instant, uncontrollable gallop. 'Stop that fool, will you, Chilla!' Blake shouted, giving chase.

They were in the land of burning water now, the mirage-haunted desert fringe. What made it worse was the unnatural heat. It was still spring.

Given the advantage, the spooked horses had all

but disappeared. The flower-strewn plains quivered and glowed in the silvery flash of the mirage, seemingly endlessly flat but actually undulating country; depressions alternating with higher ground covered in cane grass.

'They're there somewhere, and so's the stallion and his harem.' Blake called a halt.

'I'm beginning to think we won't catch him today,' said Uncle Grant.

'They'll have to come to one of the waterholes to drink.'

'I think we're in for a short, sharp shower.' Valerie lifted her cream felt hat and raked a hand through her short dark hair.

'Something tells me the stallion's not far away,' said Blake. 'What is it, Miranda?' he asked, his blue eyes resting on Miranda's creamy, flushed face.

'Nothing.' To be perfectly truthful she was aching.

'We might as well call it off, Blake,' Uncle Grant said. 'Miranda looks done in.'

'I'm not!' she protested.

'Don't take it so hard, dear,' Valerie said soothingly, 'you've kept up very well.'

'So we'll take a break,' Blake made the decision. 'You don't want to go back, do you, Miranda?'

'No, I do *not*!' She spoke emphatically, squaring her delicately determined chin.

'I wouldn't put it past you to fall out of the saddle,' said Valerie.

'Sure, if it depended on *your* support.'

Valerie flushed and looked angry, but when she went to open her mouth Blake forestalled her.

'We'll keep moving until we reach the water-hole.'

By the time they reached the eighth in the curving chain of deep waterholes they were almost beaten by the storm. It kept up in a steady fifteen-minute drumming while they huddled beneath the canopy of trees where at least a thousand birds were ruffling their wet feathers and calling to each other stridently.

'We can thank God for this,' said Blake, not the least disturbed at getting wet. 'It's a fine thing to see Morning Star in splendour,'

Swiftly the rain was gone and the storm clouds that had billowed up gave way to the hard brilliance of a peacock sky. Now, however, the air was cooler and the plains heavy with the scent of a million drenched flowers.

Miranda had her hat off and now her damp curls were clustering tightly round her face, whorls of gold that shone brightly around her small, flushed face.

'Doesn't the air smell heavenly!' she said. 'Jean Patou would love to bottle this, sell it for a small fortune an ounce, and we don't have to pay a cent!'

'I had no idea you were such a nature-lover,' commented Valerie, dismayed by the sight of the girl's indestructible young beauty. For instance, look at what the rain had done to her hair! Even her eyes were washed with brilliant colour as green as the dripping leaves. It made Valerie so angry even her voice crackled.

This time Miranda didn't answer her; nor did she appear to hear, for Blake had put out his hand

in a seemingly irresistible gesture and twined one
of those golden whorls around his finger.

'What ridiculous hair! You look like a baby.'

'Half your luck!' With Uncle Grant's shrewd
eyes on her, Valerie tried to be amusing.

'If you don't care for it,' Miranda said to Blake,
'I'll have it straightened.'

'I don't think either of us wants that. I love
babies.'

Do you? Valerie thought, inwardly fuming. If
that were true you would have married me long
ago. Damn it all, I'm *twenty-eight*, and no sweet-
faced, precocious brat is going to come between
us. It looked as if her mother had sent her over
just in time. The question was how to part them.
Blake seemed genuinely fond of the girl.

The reappearance of the little band of wild
horses cut short Valerie's speculations. They were
coming down on the northerly tip of the waterhole,
first the little filly, closely followed up by the two
colts. As yet, no friction had broken out between
the two colts. At the moment they were simply
sharing, not allowing the little filly to break up
what had been a beautiful friendship.

'Now what?' Chilla whispered in his boss's ear.

'We'll sit tight and wait.'

It didn't take long. While the three young animals were drinking, a big, nearly black stallion
materialised out of the wild bush, stood above
them on the higher ground and gave his heavy,
tangled black mane a noisy shake.

Most wild horses Miranda had seen looked fairly
harmless, but this was a powerful, formidable
animal, eyeing the colts balefully.

'Here's trouble!' Chilla hissed, and it quickly developed.

With a great snort the stallion came down on the young colts, and although they attempted to hit him from both sides they were no match for the older male. Both of them received brutal blows until they backed off, bloodied and conceding the victory. All that remained for the stallion was to pick up the filly and add her to whatever females he had already collected.

'You can bet your life that's our brute,' Blake said grimly. 'He's got good blood in him too. At a guess, Day Dawn's.' He named a stolen station mare, one of his father's great favourites and never recovered.

'Magnificent animal,' Uncle Grant murmured, 'but he looks bad.'

'That poor little filly,' Miranda said. 'I suppose he's already picked her up.'

'We'll give them time to settle then we'll see.'

Crouching low over their horses, they rode out of the trees, splashed here and there with the brilliant colour of the gorgeous ring-necked parrots.

'There they are,' Miranda whispered, pointing, when they reached the topmost slope.

'And there in the middle,' said Chilla, 'is Columbine.'

Blake tipped his stetson lower on his head. 'Six mares, the filly, three yearling colts. A fairly large band.'

'And you'll notice four of the mares and the filly are reddish-brown.' Miranda smiled wryly.

'I'm going to enjoy this!'

'Are you?' Miranda looked at Valerie quizzically.

'*I* don't want to see the stallion shot.'

'If it isn't Blake could lose more valuable mares,' Valerie pointed out rather stiffly.

'God, I think the wind's changing.' Blake cut her off.

'It seems to be.' Chilla stared at the waving branches of a delicate little menareechie. 'Damn . . . damn . . . *damn!*'

In the distance, the wild stallion lifted his arrogant head, reacting to the scents that were now carried on the breeze. For an instant he faced them in their hidden position, then he gave a snort of warning to his band.

'Spooked!' Chilla yelled disgustedly.

Herded day in and day out by the dominant male tyrant, all the animals with the exception of Columbine and the filly immediately obeyed the signal. The recalcitrant filly for her pains was savagely nipped to start her flight, but extraordinarily the stallion didn't use this technique on the beautiful chestnut mare. Instead he assumed the herding posture, weaving his fine head around for all the world like a snake.

'If he doesn't nip her soon he'll have a scattered harem.' Even Blake was surprised by this unusual display of forbearance. The rest of the band were racing madly, single file, in the direction of Walitcha, a desiccated hill that rose in a dome-shaped mound from the vast plain.

'Well, what's it to be?' Uncle Grant asked, rather wearily. 'Camp for the night and track again at first light or ride back?'

'We've come this far.' Chilla had no objection to a night under the stars. 'Seems like Columbine don't want to go.'

'And he finds her valuable enough to risk losing sight of the other mares,' Miranda whispered softly. 'Maybe there's some good in him after all.'

A few moments more and the wild stallion gave up his lenient stand. Forcible behaviour was called for, and now the mare received a painful nip that set her galloping just ahead of her abductor. Both animals were very fast, and Miranda felt her throat tighten as she watched their wild flight. So superior were they, it was evident they would overtake the brumby band in the distance.

Blake expelled a deep breath of exasperation, then turned to his uncle. 'Take the girls back and Chilla and I will go on.'

'*I'm* O.K.' Valerie's voice had a hard ring of self-assurance. 'But I expect Miranda's had enough.'

'I'm fine,' Miranda assured them.

'Frankly, I'm not,' Uncle Grant grimaced wryly. 'My back is giving me a bit of misery.'

'You should have said so.' Blake put his hand on the older man's shoulder. 'Leave now so you'll have daylight. And tell Kenny I won't need him in the morning.'

'Are you coming with me, Mirry?' Uncle Grant's blue gaze met Miranda's matter-of-factly.

'Don't be embarrassed about it, Miranda,' Valerie said kindly, 'you've done well, considering.'

As it happened Miranda had been about to say yes, not because she wanted to, but for Andrea's sake, but Valerie's smug expression put all thoughts of duty out of her head.

'If you don't mind, Uncle Grant, I haven't camped out for such a long time.'

'All right, m'dear,' Uncle Grant nodded. 'Take care, everyone.'

'You really ought to go,' Valerie protested, frowning as Uncle Grant rode away.

'It sounds as though you're trying to get rid of me!' protested Miranda.

'No, no,' Valerie said hastily, feeling Blake's brilliant eyes on her. 'I'm thinking of your well-being. You'll be awfully stiff tomorrow.'

'As it happens, Val,' Blake said smoothly, 'you're underestimating her. Miranda has always had that little extra bit in reserve.'

'Well then,' Valerie's stony expression altered to one of relief, 'I shan't worry about her any more.'

CHAPTER EIGHT

TIRED and headachey as she was, Miranda was finding it impossible to sleep. Usually a night in the softly sighing bush sent her instantly into a deep, perfect sleep, but now she turned as fretfully as though all the dingoes in creation were making the night resound with their bloodcurdling wails. Chilla's gentle snores were disturbing her, so too was the radiant white light—too strong, she felt, for sleep. The sunset, hours before, had been a gold and crimson glory, yet it didn't have the excitement of this ghostly, gleaming white light.

'Blake?' she whispered to the lean figure close at hand.

'Don't tell me, you can't sleep.'

'No,' she sighed gently, leaning towards him so she wouldn't disturb Valerie, who had gone out like a light.

'Silly little chick!' He stretched out his hand as though to an overtired child, but as their hands met and joined Miranda recognised instantly what was the matter with her. She wanted the comfort and ultimately the danger of contact with Blake's body. 'Come over here,' he said soothingly.

'My head aches.' She went to lie down beside him.

'Grant told you to go home with him instead of chasing after me.'

'I'm not chasing after you!' she hissed wrath-fully.

'Aren't you?' His exact expression was hidden from her, but his eyes were glittering like diamonds. 'Here, lie on my shoulder.'

'Just listen to Chilla snoring!' she smiled.

'The sleep of exhaustion.' He put his arm around her, fitting her to his side. 'I think I even detected a few snores from Val.'

'God, I thought she was too disciplined.' Under her ear, his heart was beating strongly. 'I think I'd better go back to my own pozzie before morning. You've got one jealous woman there.'

'Be quiet!'

'All right.' She nuzzled her head several times before she found the most comfortable position.

'Are you quite through?'

'Goodnight, Blake,' she whispered.

'Night, flower face.'

For a time both of them lay there in silence while waves and waves of unrest swept through Miranda's softly curving body. When she was a child Blake had always possessed a unique magic for her; the magic of comfort, but now she had fallen in love.

'The moonlight's spookey, don't you think?'

'Shut up!' There was no mistaking the tone or the taut impatience of his body.

An unseen night bird dropped three notes into the still air; sweet, clear, liquid notes.

'What bird is that?' Miranda lifted her chin and her mouth grazed his throat.

'Are you going to settle down?' His warm breath stirred her curls.

'I don't think so. I feel odd.'

'Ah!' He lay back against the saddle he was using as a headrest.

'I'm always talking when I'm not supposed to,' she sighed.

'I think you'll be wretched until I kiss you to sleep.'

'You're crazy!' It was a reproachful little quaver.

'So you keep saying.' His hand closed under her chin and lifted it. 'It so happens, Miranda, I know you.'

'What happens if Valerie wakes up?' she threatened him.

'We won't make a sound.'

His warm mouth claimed hers, gently at first, almost teasing, then when it opened under his, convulsively as though he had only been tormenting her. Now his body turned towards hers and he hauled her against him so her small, yielding figure knew every inch of his hard frame.

Madness!

Streams of sensation were setting Miranda alight. Now Blake lifted her so she was lying on top of him, a fragile weight, then down on the rug at the other side while his broad back shielded her from the other sleeping forms.

Her mind registered that she mustn't cry out, if he ever freed her mouth, but then his hand unbuttoned her shirt and found her naked breast.

'Blake!' Her whole body convulsed and tears spurted to her eyes. She had truly never known she was a woman before.

'You belong to me.' It was just above a breath,

but with so much feeling in it, it drew her heart out.

'No.' Still she refused to admit it, even when her writhing body was betraying her enslavement.

'I want to make you suffer a little,' he muttered.

Could there be a better way? With her body clamped to his, a willing victim, his hand cupping and lifting her tender breasts, she knew an eroticism in herself that had hitherto been concealed. Now it was she who was pressing herself against him with total abandonment, feeling every movement of his strong male body.

'Tell me. Tell my why,' she begged him.

'What was your first fiancé's name?' he bit out in a strange voice.

'Do you really expect me to remember?'

Clothes now were an impediment. She was blind to her surroundings, kissed and caressed to the point where her bodily demands were too urgent. She desperately wanted Blake to take her. It couldn't be otherwise, from the hard rasp in his voice. Why did he want her so badly? It was strange.

So much pressure was building up inside her it was dizzying. Her eyelids fluttered as he raised her body and brought her breasts on line with his mouth. Now his hands dug in at her waist and she buried her face in the crisp waves of his hair, perfectly still with a terrible tension as his mouth hungrily teased her.

Then she was overwhelmed; by him, by herself, melting inside so he could have done anything he liked. All was desire, a bottomless black well in which she was desperate to drown. The more he wanted of her, the more she had to give, but she was trapped inside her clothes.

She must have nearly fainted, for he was above her, propped up on an elbow, looking down. 'Don't faint on me,' he whispered.

'No.' It sounded very soft and weak.

'I expect I want too much of you.' His forefinger traced the outline of her softly pulsing lips. 'Some time I'm going to take you, Miranda. You know that.'

'I want it *now*.'

'Not this way.'

'What's happening to me, Blake?' She looked up into his eyes.

'I've felt like this for a long time.'

'Since when?' She was shocked.

'That's hard to say. Let's face it, darling, there's not much you weren't blessed with.' His lean brown fingers stroked her breasts until she shivered, then he rebuttoned her thin cotton shirt. 'You're so sweet! God, you have no idea. I'll have to make love to you more often. That way we'll correct your tendency to faint on me.'

'You sound as if you despise yourself.'

'I didn't plan to want you, Miranda,' he said sombrely. 'It just happened.'

'I'm sorry.' She lifted her arm and bent it across her forehead. 'I suppose you think I'm some kind of threat to you?'

'I know you are.' He lifted her arm away, pinning one, then the other above her head. 'I've always been your teacher in everything. That's why you couldn't give yourself to anyone else.'

'So there's nothing to be done?'

'No.' He looked down at her, her pearly face and the exquisite rounded breasts, running the length of her so that she felt flushed and impassioned. 'How fortunate that we're not alone. It's the surest way to control.'

'How do you do it?' she said bitterly.

'The way it might turn out. I wouldn't really hurt you, Miranda. Just a little.' He lowered his head as if to kiss her again, and just at that moment Valerie stirred in her sleep, turned over on her right side and muttered aloud Blake's name.

'Hell!' Miranda gave an hysterical little sob. 'I think you owe it to Val to marry her.'

'And she has so much materially to offer. Whereas you have nothing.' He fell back again, resting his dark head against the saddle. 'Come here and shut up.'

'Thank you.' She felt humiliated but obliged to stay. 'There's no need to put your arm around me.'

'If you don't like it, go some place else.'

But of course, Miranda didn't.

In the shadowy light of pre-dawn Blake came awake, easing Miranda's silky, scented head gently off his shoulder. She was deeply asleep, whereas he had slept badly, snatching minutes here and there.

'Boss?' Chilla's hoarse whisper reached him.

'Get yourself together and we'll ride out. If there's going to be any danger, I don't want the girls in the way.'

'No, sir!' Chilla gave the impression that having women around really pained him.

Birds converging on the sheet of clear water stirred Miranda to life. She sat up quickly, staring around her, but the men were gone. Only Valerie was there at the water's edge, splashing her face and throat.

'Damn it, they've gone!' Miranda called quite loudly.

'All your fault!' Heavy-eyed and rather haggard, Valerie strode back to her, wiping her face with her red bandana. 'No doubt Blake was worried about his wee lamb.'

'Has something in particular upset you?' For a terrible moment Miranda thought Valerie might have actually seen them.

'Why did you come, Miranda? Making a nuisance of yourself.'

'Well, I'm certainly bugging you,' Miranda sighed.

'And you know why!' Valerie made a choked sound. 'I'm all for getting down to basics, and it seems to me you've launched yourself on a little flirtation with Blake. I can't think of it humorously—it sticks in my throat.'

'I can see that.' Miranda stood up and folded the rug, and a new expression leapt into Valerie's eyes.

'You know damned well you were on the other side of the fire last night!'

'So I shifted.'

Valerie looked at her with anger and suspicion in her eyes. 'So you could be beside Blake?'

'I rather wish you'd stop, Valerie,' Miranda said tiredly. 'I don't have to ask your permission about anything and I shouldn't have thought Blake has to either.'

For answer Valerie stepped forward and gripped Miranda's arm. 'It's a dreadful thing you're doing.

Blake belongs to me!'

Miranda looked down at Valerie's strong hand. 'Would you *mind*?'

'Mother said you were up to something.' Valerie made no effort to release her. 'What's wrong, Miranda? Your latest little affair didn't work out, so now you've turned your big eyes on Blake.'

Miranda pulled away violently. 'Any bachelor's fair game until he's safely married, or at the very least engaged.'

'We've discussed it,' Valerie said emotionally.

'And?' Miranda's fair skin was clearly showing the imprint of Valerie's strong fingers.

'And he loves me.'

'Then he'd do well to put a ring on your finger. If I were you, Valerie, I'd issue an ultimatum. Marriage or nothing—one or the other.'

'Ah, then, but I have more style!'

'Then you'll stay ringless. Men understand very well when you mean business. After all, you're what? In your late twenties? You'd be silly to waste any more time.'

'And you can mind your own business!' Valerie picked up her hat and crammed it down on her head.

'I'd be equally pleased if you could do the same thing yourself. It's rather tedious being treated like a naughty child.'

'I think you are,' snapped Valerie.

'Then you're a fool.'

With an angry shake of her head Valerie picked up her saddle and streaked up the bank. She was amazingly fit and strong, and Miranda too shook her head ruefully and walked down to the shining

sheet of water. Had Blake really discussed marriage
with Valerie? Miranda was certain he wasn't passionately in love with her, but maybe passion had
nothing to do with the marriages of the very rich.
Blake had said so himself. Valerie had a great deal
to offer. There was Kanimbla and all that went
with it; a half-way point between Morning Star and
Charlotte Downs, Seymour property in the north
of the State. Though Morning Star had access to
permanent water in the worst times of drought,
cattle could be very easily moved along the chain.

Behind her, Valerie in the saddle slapped the
rump of Miranda's sensitive mare, who immediately tore away, affronted.

'You stupid. . . .' Miranda wheeled grimly, staring up the bank.

'It should be a long walk home,' drawled Valerie.

'What do you think Blake will say?'

'But I had nothing to do with it,' Valerie
laughed. 'Do you think *I* would ever do such a
thing? You were just going to saddle up the mare
when something spooked her and she bolted.'

'You're not concerned that the wild stallion
might sight the mare?'

'He won't.' Valerie gave a thin smile. 'And even
if he does, it was your fault.'

'And I thought you loved horses, 'Miranda said
disgustedly. 'All right, off you go. You're a big girl
in the saddle, but as far as I'm concerned you're a
pain in the neck out of it!'

So now she was on her own. There was no use
trying to get the mare back. Valerie would no
doubt drive it off in the direction of the home
yards. What a stupid thing to do! Infantile.

Miranda splashed her face in the stream, luxuriating, in spite of herself, in its cold, crystal freshness. This was an important watering place. Someone would pick her up. But when? She scooped up handful after handful of water and splashed it on her face until it was gleaming like tinted satin. There were the most beautiful little coloured stones in the water, shimmering like gemstones, and she reached for them, stuffing them in her every pocket. Andrea with her instinctive eye for colour and texture should love them. Perhaps they had been used for some ceremony and later discarded. There were so many of them.

As she put them in her breast pocket she shivered, hardly believing that Blake had claimed her there with his hands and his mouth. Could anyone ever explain how one man's caresses were heaven and another's completely unacceptable? She felt the same emotion now, only now she was simply frightened of it. The possibility that Blake would take her as he wanted had to be faced. She wanted it too, the absolute ecstasy, but wouldn't life be empty after? Desire didn't always make for happiness, and in committing herself even once to Blake she could be exposing herself to a lifetime sensation of loss. A woman gave so much when she gave herself. For it to have any meaning there had to be mutual respect. Before any man took her, Miranda decided, in the brilliant daylight, they would first have to say *I love you* and mean it. Of course moonlight was a different thing. One forgot everything.

'Oh, damn you, Blake!' she cried aloud, and her cry of anguish startled the birds. They took off from the trees in an explosion of colour, startlingly bright against the living green.

On the other side of the water, a beautiful kangaroo was staring across at her. Plainly he didn't know what to do; drink, or make a bolt for it. Miranda remained exactly where she was, trying to project fellowship. The kangaroo still stood tall, staring, then apparently satisfied she meant no harm, lowered his head to the stream. It was a delightful study and Miranda was sorry she didn't have her camera. Maybe she could interest Andrea in photography; she should be able to with an Instamatic. Any baby thing was pretty, little joeys peeping out of their mother's pouch, and baby emus were delightful, with their greyish-white, black-striped plumage. Many the time she had seen a mob of these birds, the second largest in the world, streaking across the plains. When she was little, there had even been a station pet that followed everyone around like a puppy. Andrea had no pets, which in Miranda's opinion was a serious lack. Justine was no animal lover, but she shouldn't deprive her child.

Miranda waited at the camp site an hour, then she was drawn to explore the plain. By now Stuart had probably classified dozens of new plants and because he was such a nice man she had the warm feeling that he would have shown his drawings and specimens to Andrea. She had accepted him easily, united by a common bond. Both were artists, ever observant of the tiniest little thing.

Only wisps of the blue mirage were shimmering across the flats. Later, as the sun ascended to its zenith, all manner of phenomena would be thrown up; hills and lakes and strange castles, transforming the landscape. Sometimes the illusions were so strong one could ride almost into them before they broke up; whole quicksilver scenes. That could be a mob of four or five hundred cattle in the distance or it could be the mirage. No sound reverberated on the air and sound carried far.

What a situation! She could be waiting for hours. Still, there were compensations. Her senses were assaulted by colour and the great silence. There was so much peace here; so much fulfilment. She really did have an affinity with nature.

Miranda walked along, glorying in the wilderness. She felt so tiny in this mind-boggling landscape, but strangely not unimportant. A huge cloud of budgerigars blazed across the sky, stirring her interest, and but for this she could have walked by a newborn foal without noticing him. His reddish-brown coat blended perfectly with the desert sand and Miranda stared down incredulously, scarcely able to believe her eyes.

'Oh, you beautiful little thing!' There he was, camouflaged by the glowing sand and the blazing scarlet of a desert bush. 'You darling little thing!' She dropped to her knees, fascinated by the baby. She had seen many newborn foals before, but the miracle was still the same.

'Where's your mamma?' She looked about her for an animal pad. Though well hidden the little foal seemed very vulnerable. 'She has to be around here some place.' Perhaps she belonged to the mahogany stallion and had been separated from the band by the birth? Either way, Miranda considered, she was in a little bit of trouble if the mare came back. She would never expect to find a human bent over her precious son.

Miranda backed away and sat down in the shelter of a great clump of saltbush. Any moment she expected to see the mother horse loom into sight, but though she remained where she was among the fragrant flowers, the mare did not return. Was she sick? Dead? No mare with a new foal would return to the band. Even a tyrant like the-mahogany stallion would wait patiently for her return. Sometimes this could take months. There were rules even in the wilds, so where was the mare?

Finally Miranda decided to try and locate her. She must be in trouble, otherwise she would never have deserted her foal. So far the little creature hadn't even bothered to stand, though it would have been able to do so shortly after birth.

Near the waterhole, almost hidden by the cane-grass, Miranda found the bay mare. She was in extremity, and Miranda's eyes filled with tears.

'Poor old girl!'

The mare had run wild all her life. She had never heard a human voice or felt a human hand, yet she lifted her head as though she recognised that here was comfort. Slowly, protected by her compassion and the mare's dying state, Miranda drew nearer. What she wanted to do was cradle the mare's head, but she feared the fright would be too much. Instead she sat down some little way off, talking quietly, telling the mare *she* would accept responsibility for the foal. The mare might never have understood, but there was no doubt she derived some comfort from this human communication. Miranda had always talked to horses, now it stood her in good stead. While the mare died she kept up a gentle, soothing flow, but afterwards she bowed her head in her hands and cried.

When Blake found her she was sitting among the flowers with the foal's head in her lap.

'My God!' He was soon out of the saddle, looking around him for a furious mother horse.

'It's all right.' Miranda didn't even lift her head. 'She's dead.'

'Oh!' He let out a strangled breath. 'Where have you been? I've been nearly out of my mind!'

Only then did Miranda lift her tear-streaked face. 'I promised the mare I'd look after her colt.'

'All right.' He put out his hand and brushed the tears from her cheeks.

'I dared not move lest I frighten him. He seems so weak.'

'I'll take him, miss.' Chilla was beside them, his normally gravelly voice beautifully gentle. 'Nice little fella. He's hungry.'

'Come on, Miranda.' Free of the foal, Blake lifted her up. 'We're going home.'

Valerie was there, sitting her horse, staring down at them. 'You didn't ask us if we found the stallion.'

'You must have.' Miranda glanced at her only briefly. 'I see you have Columbine.'

'Had to shoot him, miss,' Chilla told her. 'It was the only way we were gunna recover the mare.'

'Oh.' Beyond that, Miranda offered no comment. Blake was ruthless when it came to protecting his property.

Listlessly she allowed him to settle her before

him, missing the glittering look Valerie swept over them. Did anything go as planned?

'Don't worry about the foal,' Blake told Miranda quietly. 'He's got a good chance.'

'I'm going to let Andrea help me.' Miranda relaxed against him, mesmerised by his nearness. 'She's terrified of horses, I know, but a little foal is something else again.'

'Right.' Apparently he was going to agree with anything she said. 'Ten minutes ago I was furiously angry and worried. Now I feel no such thing.' His arm tightened about her, and only then did Miranda realise there was a tremor behind the iron strength.

Andrea's reception of the little orphan was everything Miranda could have wanted.

'Can I touch him?' she whispered, round-eyed.

'You can feed him.' Miranda looked seriously down at the child.

'*Feed* him?' Andrea couldn't believe her ears.

'It's our responsibility to look after him, yours and mine,' Miranda told her.

'I always do the wrong thing. I might *hurt* him,' Andrea said mournfully.

'You won't,' Miranda replied promptly. 'I'll show you how, then we can take it in turns.'

'I get afraid sometimes, Manda.'

'Yes, darling,' Miranda drew the child to her and put an arm around her. 'We all do. But we go on trying. I'll be here. I'll show you, and the little foal is so hungry he'll understand what you're trying to do. Help him. Help him stay alive. Remember, it's up to us.'

'Show me,' Andrea said with a dawning sense of responsibility. 'Honestly, he's so *lovely*!'

It was a miracle of a sort, for it marked the beginning of the end of Andrea's fear of horses. From then on the little foal held a great fascination for her, and no child could have cared for it more devotedly. For a time she lived at the stables, and Justine wasn't going to allow this to pass without stinging comment.

'I suppose I'll have to resign myself now to my daughter being a horse person.'

They were seated at the dinner table and Uncle Grant flushed angrily. 'Andrea doesn't seem to do anything you approve of!'

So unexpected was his attack, Justine seemed faintly at a loss. Why, Grant never criticised her about anything.

'So far as I'm concerned,' he continued, 'it's little short of a miracle. Surely you can see that?'

Justine bit her lip and looked down.

'I would like to say too,' Uncle Grant looked rather sternly around the table, 'in front of everyone, how grateful I am to Miranda for her splendid understanding. I think she's the gentlest creature I've ever known, and she's shown us, Justine and myself, just how wrong we've been about our own child. Far from being slow, which we'd somehow, God knows why, accepted, Andrea is an exceptionally gifted child. Stuart before he left urged me get her started on art lessons. Justine, you could do that. After all, it's from you that she's inherited her ability.'

'So that's to be my new role in life?' Justine stood up so abruptly she almost sent her chair over.

'Tutoring a four-year-old! I don't know why you're all so impressed with her scrawls. Obviously you have little idea of real talent!'

'Obviously,' said Blake very dryly. 'Observe our art collection.'

'So you've got tons of money and good taste. I wish you could compare my early drawings with those of Andrea's, then you'd see why I can't get worked up about a series of over-vivid scrawls. They're ugly and undisciplined and they clearly show that Andrea is a disturbed child.'

'You don't accept any responsibility?' Blake asked quietly, but his light eyes were steely.

'No! No! *No!* Why turn on me, Blake? You know I've done everything I can.'

'Please sit down again, Justine,' Gran requested formally, looking all of a sudden very old and tired. 'We realise you've been deeply unhappy about Andrea.'

'Andrea!' Justine pressed her hands together and stared up sightlessly at the richly decorated plaster ceiling. Tears sparkled in her eyes and Uncle Grant stood up and put his arms around her.

'Please, dear, let me take you upstairs.'

'Oh, go to hell!' Justine broke away from him and fled from the room.

No one looked after her. Gran bent her head, distressed; Blake's striking dark face took on a look of bitter cynicism, Uncle Grant looked deeply hurt and embarrassed and Miranda, like Gran, kept her golden head bent over her long-stemmed crystal wine glass.

'I think you can say,' Uncle Grant remarked to no one in particular, 'my marriage is a disaster.'

'The blame is not entirely due to you,' Blake remarked with bitter humour. 'Why don't you have it out now?'

'What would you suggest I do?' Uncle Grant turned to his nephew with a sigh.

'I think I'd slap her.'

She'd be pleased about that, Miranda thought, and as she lifted her eyes she caught an identical expression in Gran's eyes. Of course Gran knew. Blake *had* to, otherwise he would have been very blind indeed. Justine was raving mad about him. The only one who didn't seem to know was Uncle Grant, who would probably never break out of his bachelor euphoria.

'Why don't you do as I suggested?' Gran reached for a sip of wine to fortify herself. 'Take her away for a time. Andrea will be perfectly all right here.'

'Damn it all, Mother, I don't want to. I've had my trotting around the world.'

'Do you want to save your marriage?' Blake challenged him rather brutally, Miranda thought.

'Dear God!' Uncle Grant was surprised anyone should think he was less than attentive. 'Could a trip away guarantee Justine happiness? I never dreamed it would be like this.'

'What are you going to do about it, then?' Blake asked with more ease than he felt. 'Living on Morning Star isn't enough for Justine. She should never have been taken away from the city.'

'I told her what it was going to be like,' Uncle Grant slumped down defeatedly into his chair. 'She was anxious to come then. God help me, wasn't she? I suppose at best I'm a terrible husband.'

'Perhaps you never looked at each other properly,' said Gran. 'It's very difficult when one doesn't share the same interests. Justine is not at all a countrywoman, neither has she really accepted parenthood. Perhaps her temperament goes along with her gift—and she *is* gifted. That big abstract in her bedroom is superb.'

'What a pity her husband's not.' Uncle Grant put out a hand and Blake passed him the wine bottle. 'I'm not really a marvellous success at anything.'

'Dear boy——' Gran looked upset. 'You're being very hard on yourself.'

'Nevertheless that's my image of myself. I'll see where Justine wants to go and I'll take her. As though galloping off in all directions will solve the problem.'

So Uncle Grant gritted his teeth and prepared to leave Morning Star for a time.

But it wasn't going to be as simple as that. Hours later, when she should have been asleep, Miranda went downstairs with the intention of finding a good book to wallow in. Usually after a chapter or two she dozed off with the thing in her hands. Uncle Grant's depression had got to them all. Gran had even asked for a little brandy to help her sleep soundly.

The house was never left entirely in darkness. There were always a few wall brackets left on so people wouldn't stumble over and kill themselves. Magnificent as the house was, a vast collection of antiques bedevilled even the inmates, let alone guests. It struck Miranda suddenly that she loved the house like this, the golden gloom. It transformed everything so that the different views were very deep and mysterious.

The sound of a voice issuing from Blake's study brought her to a shocked halt. It was Justine, and what she was saying made every nerve in Miranda's body jump.

'I want to hate you, Blake, but I *can't*!'

'Isn't the next step for you to tell me you love me?'

'You're such a cynical bastard, aren't you?' Justine cried, impassioned. 'Have you ever loved any woman?'

'There's only one that's got a hold on me.'

'I knew it!'

The triumph in Justine's voice literally made Miranda jump.

'I'm yours for the taking, Blake. I have been from the day I came into this house.'

'Hold it!' Blake sounded so brutal, Miranda cringed. 'You've got it all wrong, Justine. You've never been anything to me but Grant's wife.'

'Don't get angry,' she begged him. 'I know it's a terrible situation, but we can work it out. Grant is a decent man. He won't hold me to a marriage I don't want.'

'What was the all-enveloping emotion you felt when you married him?' Blake asked, and his vibrant voice was harsh. 'Greed? Don't think I haven't checked out your background. Why, you've never even allowed your parents to see their only grandchild.'

'You *didn't*!' Justine's husky voice sounded suffused with tears.

'I don't understand you, Justine,' Blake said,

cold) flat and hard. 'Love I know already. What I feel for you is pity.'

'*Brute!*' Justine screeched so loudly, Miranda permitted herself to intervene. She rushed to the slightly ajar study door, pushed it in, then leant back against it to close it fast.

'Can't you keep your voice down? I'd hate Uncle Grant to burst in on all this.'

'Who cares?' Justine laughed violently.

'Have no fear, Miranda,' Blake said acidly, 'it's all over.'

'Is it?' Justine turned on him, a dramatic figure in the most beautiful and most revealing nightgown and matching peignoir Miranda had ever seen. 'You can't deny you feel something for me. I've seen you watching me. I'm not a fool. I know when a man desires me.'

'This family is falling to bits!' Miranda groaned, and put both hands to her aching temples.

'Who asked you to interfere?' Justine's exotic face was a stony mask. 'Little Miss Miranda. *Usurper!*'

'Believe what you want,' Miranda said tiredly, 'I'm going back upstairs.'

'Don't,' Blake said wryly, 'I couldn't stand it.'

'Then stop it and tell her you don't love her,' Miranda suggested.

'God!' Blake muttered witheringly. 'Do you women do anything but read books? Justine has set her heart on an illicit romance and I'm the poor mug she's decided she loves. It struck her like a bolt from the blue immediately she stepped inside this house. In fact she's been seething with passion for the past five years.'

Miranda was humiliated on Justine's account. 'Oh, don't, Blake,' she said imploringly. 'You always did have an acid tongue.'

'I'm sorry.' Blake bowed ironically. 'I wish I could be sweet about it, I really do.'

Miranda winced delicately, but Justine threw out her arms. 'You don't have to pretend, Blake. You can't be blamed. Things happen. We don't decide who we love. Why do you think Valerie went off so abruptly? It finally got through to her that you don't give a damn.'

'And about time,' he said sardonically.

'What did you tell her?' Miranda, too, remembered the way Valerie had gone off.

'Nothing much.' His silvery glance struck Miranda's little-girl-ready-for-bed face. 'I told her I'm going ahead with my plans to marry somebody else.'

'You're *what*?' Justine went so white Miranda thought she was about to pass out.

'Most people do it.' Blake came closer to Miranda and put his hands on her shoulders. 'The fact is, Justine, Miranda is my dream girl. She has been for quite a while.'

'You're mad!' Had Justine had a dagger she would have plunged it in Miranda's heart.

'You don't fancy the idea?' he asked coolly. 'Gran will be thrilled.'

'I don't believe this!' Justine made a frenzied turn about the room. 'Miranda's just a child!'

Miranda was so stunned she wasn't even aware of her immediate surroundings.

'No, really——' Blake said dryly. 'She's almost twenty-one.'

'He's joking, isn't he?' Justine looked at the stricken Miranda just as helplessly.

'I think he's serious,' she said slowly. It didn't take much figuring out. Justine's mad passion had to be terminated, so she, Miranda, had been elected to take care of it.

'I think I'll have to lie down,' Justine muttered.

Blake went promptly to the door and held it open. 'Do the sensible thing, Justine, and wipe the whole thing from your mind. I promise you I will.'

She went past him without a word, as pallid as a zombie.

'So that's taken care of very nicely.'

'I sure hope so!' Blake said almost violently. 'Two women in the one week—God, it's too much!'

'Poor you!' Miranda sank dazedly into the embrace of a big black leather armchair. 'To think of all the females who've been taken in by your charm!'

'Most days I react unfavourably towards females,' he told her. He walked to his desk, picked up a book and suddenly hurled it at the wall. 'What a farce!'

'Poor Justine,' Miranda shook her head. 'She'll hate you now.'

'I think I prefer it in her more than anyone I know. If it wasn't so damned ridiculous it would be horrible. I hope Grant takes her abroad and dumps her there.'

'What *is* he going to do?' Miranda looked up at Blake's tall, lean figure, the brilliant, blazing eyes. 'Afterwards, I mean. It would be just as bad Justine hating you as loving you. It's all so embarrassing.'

'Admittedly.' Blake's look of intolerable disgust gave way to a wry amusement. 'Anyway, by then we'll be married.'

'I have my own plans!' Miranda announced, suddenly infuriated by his arrogance.

'Really? What are they?' He appeared to be amused by the crispness in her voice.

'I don't believe I have to tell you.'

'Oh yes, you do.' From violent exasperation he was crisp and cool and in control.

'You're a dictator, Blake!' she said recklessly.

'A damned nice one to you.' His eyes flickered over her, causing her breathing to become urgent and deeper. 'What could be more suitable for the master of Morning Star than an exquisite twenty-year-old virgin?'

'I could be totally putting you on.'

'No, baby,' he shook his dark head. 'You've been addicted to me for years.'

'Have I?' She was anxious to put him straight. 'I've only known I've been in love with you for a little while.'

'Because up until now you've been a scared little rabbit.'

'Rabbit?' The colour rushed up under her skin and she started out of her chair. 'I'm a strong-minded adult!'

'Not yet.' One hand reached out for her and closed at her waist. 'But you're well on the way.'

'Touch me and you'll be sorry!' Miranda exploded, not even knowing why she was so furiously angry.

'What would you do?' Blake looked down at her with interested eyes.

'I won't be ordered round for the rest of my life!'

'It's not as bad as that.'

'It is!' She hated him when he had that glittery, arrogant look.

'All right,' he released her suddenly. 'Do I take it I'm being refused?'

'You can't expect me to believe you're serious,' she protested. 'You just want me for protection.'

'And you can't even do me this little favour?'

'Until when?' She realised some drastic step was necessary. The sooner Justine started to forget Blake, the better.'

'I don't know. Fifty years? More for you.'

'Be serious, Blake!' She begged.

'I am,' he said smoothly, shrugging one powerful shoulder. 'If Morning Star is to have an heir I have to get married, and you're considerably prettier than anyone else I know.'

'I can't take this in,' Miranda said dazedly.

'Shall I help you out?' The bright insolence was on him again, the knowledge that he had only to touch her.

'That won't settle anything,' she said shakily

'It's damned difficult not to!' His eyes swept her face and the tender curves of her girl's body. Light probed her shell-pink robe, pointing up the high tilt of her breasts, the narrow waist and the delicate bones of her hips. 'Just the sight of you is enough to make me catch my breath.'

His vibrant voice went suddenly husky, and Miranda shut her eyes. Everything about Blake made her very, very vulnerable, yet what she wanted to hear he would probably never say. What came first with Blake was the station—the station's needs. He had a nerve, calling her pretty. She'd been told dozens of times she was beautiful. The most shocking part of it all was that she wanted him so badly—teasing, tormenting, dictatorial Blake.

The feel of his hands on her caused her to cry out aloud. 'Oh, don't kiss me,' she begged him. 'Do . . o . . n't!'

His mouth closed over the frenzied, murmured word, the heat of his body igniting her own.

'Poor baby!' He was kissing her hungrily all over her face. 'When are you going to sleep with me?'

'Never!' Now her throat was being assailed, beneath her ear.

'You will. You can't help it.'

'I don't understand anything,' she wailed. 'You don't even propose! You dictate.'

He laughed in his throat and lifted her like a pirate bent on ravishment. 'Miranda, little flower, won't you please marry me?'

'I have to speak to Gran.'

'What, now?' He had her cradled in his lap.

'I wouldn't disturb her for nothing, but this is important.'

He seized her blonde head with his two hands. 'Settle down. You don't have to check with Gran. She thinks you're perfect.' His dark voice was heavily spiked with mockery and hearing it, Miranda started to cry.

'Oh, damn you, Blake. *Damn* you!' Her voice broke.

'Don't cry,' he said with unexpected violence.

'Why not?' She dashed a hand across her cheek.

'Because if you do,' he stared down at her,' I'll lose all control.'

It was baffling. He couldn't mean it. No woman had that much power over Blake. She felt as if she was out in a terrible storm, afraid of the lightning.

'Then I'd better not.' She touched the tip of her tongue to her mouth and tasted the salt of her own tears. The action was innocent, instinctive, yet it had a galvanic effect on him. She had long enough to catch the flash in his eyes, then her head was strained back over his shoulder and his mouth bore down on hers with the primitive need to reduce her to yielding flesh.

It was desperate, urgent, and there weren't any words. Now her breasts were barely covered and when his fingers sought out the nipple she betrayed herself into sighing voluptuously, her soft, yearning body shuddering involuntarily.

'You know I'm crazily in love with you, don't you?'

'*No*!' She arched her body while he caressed her.

'You damned well know it,' he said harshly.

Did she know it? *Did* she?

'Tell me you love me,' she begged him.

'I've waited for years for you to grow up.' He twisted her head up to him again.

It was incredible, but he was very pale under his dark tan. 'But all those other women?' she asked incredulously.

'Did I mention your two fiancés?' Blake tugged teasingly on her silky curls.

'But I thought. . . .' her green eyes were almost swallowing up her face. 'We all thought it was Val

for sure. She even told me you had an arrangement.'

'Never!'

'But you've kissed her, made love to her.'

'I honestly don't remember.'

'You *must*!' The words burst from her.

'I was never her lover.' A kind of impatience
prowled in his brilliant eyes. 'What I mean is, Miranda, you have no cause to be jealous of anyone.'

'I'm not jealous,' she said truthfully. 'God knows
why I'm not, but I'm not.'

'It isn't enough for me to say I love you?' There
was tension in his caressing hand.

'I can't help feeling sorry for a lot of people,'
Miranda sighed.

'One of the reasons I love you, your sweetness,
compassion. . . .'

She looked quickly into his eyes and the deep
sincerity was there now, no longer hidden or
masked.

'What else do you want me to say?' Blake asked
a little wryly.

'Nothing.' She put up a slender arm and wound
it around his neck. 'I've no aim in life but to be
everything you want.'

'Mine everlasting,' he said with tender triumph.
'Nothing would have meaning without you.' He
held her quietly for a moment longer, but then their
emotions became too strong. His lips found her
eyelids, her temples, the hollow at the base of her
throat, then when she could stand it no longer, her
mouth.

On her twenty-first birthday Miranda and Blake

were married. Lucy was her matron of honour and two of her best friends from her student days made ravishingly pretty bridesmaids. Though it was common knowledge now that Grant Seymour's (some said ill-advised) marriage had broken up, his little daughter Andrea was plainly thrilled to be flower-girl. Of course Manda and Blake were going away on their honeymoon, she had been told, but it didn't matter. They were coming back.

Andrea, a poised little figure in her beautiful long blue dress, held tightly to her father's hand and waved them off.

THE AUSTRALIAN DINGO

When European explorers first visited Australia, they were captivated by its bizarre creatures. Not surprisingly, however, their reports back to the Old World were scorned. Surely an animal that carries its young in a pouch must be a mythical creature!

But there was one animal that did not have to be seen to be believed: Australia's wild dog, the dingo.

Some anthropologists believe the dingo is the world's oldest canine. It is a member of the wolf family—the only Australian animal belonging to that family—but unlike the wolf, it does not travel in packs. Generally it forages alone or in the company of a partner, hiding by day, hunting by night, and collectively taking an annual multimillion-dollar toll on flocks of sheep and cattle. The dingo also hunts kangaroos and rabbits and has been seen catching birds on the wing. Attacks on humans are rare, though Margaret Way's heroine, Miranda, was an unfortunate victim!

The dingo is usually sandy in color. It has a blunt head, short ears and a bushy tail with white markings on the tip. It howls...long and painfully.

Although this wild dog still covers a wide territory, it no longer roams as freely over the Australian outback as it once did. Control measures include trapping, poisoning and even the erection of a "dingo fence," which stretches for thousands of miles from Queensland to South Australia. In most states there is a bounty on the unpopular dingo, but control remains difficult because dingoes are highly reproductive, a female giving birth to as many as nine pups a year.

Your FREE gift includes

- *Anne Hampson* — Beyond the Sweet Waters
- *Anne Mather* — The Arrogant Duke
- *Violet Winspear* — Cap Flamingo
- *Nerina Hilliard* — Teachers Must Learn

FREE GIFT CERTIFICATE

and Subscription Reservation

Mail this coupon today!

In the U.S.A.
1440 South Priest Drive
Tempe, AZ 85281

In Canada
649 Ontario Street
Stratford, Ontario N5A 6W2

Harlequin Reader Service:

Please send me my 4 Harlequin Romance novels FREE.
Also, reserve a subscription to the 6 NEW Harlequin
Romance novels published each month. Each month I will
receive 6 NEW Romance novels at the low price of $1.50
each (*Total–$9.00 a month*). There are no shipping and
handling or any other hidden charges. I may cancel this
arrangement at any time, but even if I do, these first 4 books
are still mine to keep.

NAME   (PLEASE PRINT)

ADDRESS

CITY   STATE/PROV.   ZIP/POSTAL CODE

Offer expires January 31, 1983
Offer not valid to present subscribers.   S2490

Prices subject to change without notice.